Echoes of a Boy

Richard Godfray-Hoare

DEDICATION

To myself, age 17, keep going with your dreams. I know for a fact one day you will live the life you desire and get to see Murder at St Philip's finally published, in one form or another. The journey will not always be easy, but the destination is worth putting in the miles for, trust me.

To everyone else I have ever known, whether mentioned in these pages or not, you have all played a role in shaping both my life and this story. Thank you.

PREFACE

It's dark. It never seems as bad in the summer but it's January, so it's dark. I think it's the central heating that stirred me, two weeks off work should have reset the body clock a little. I think it's probably the heating, maybe the dog. Three snooze buttons to go!

I creep from the bedroom by the light of my iPhone and the morning ritual begins again, like riding the proverbial bike. Pee first, I'm fifty after all. Wash, dress, feed the dog. The dog is more clockwork than me so as soon as he's eaten, he is out into the garden for his own morning ablutions. This gives me time to make a flask of coffee for the commute. Doggie business done, quick pat on the head and then I'm off down the garden path, the dog is probably back upstairs on the bed before I get to the car.

Not the most wintery of days, so no de-icing required but the windscreen's a little misted so, while the car warms, I continue the rituals and plug the phone into the charger and take a sip of coffee as Nicky Campbell, not for the first time, becomes the opening voice of my day.

The commute is just a little short of sixty miles but perfectly doable. The occasional accident aside, it's a ninety-minute trip. It should be quicker but West Oxfordshire District Council are only just set to begin the A40 road improvements after decades of road surveys and procrastinations. No big holdups today though and I'm in the office by 8am.

When I say, 'I'm in the office', I literally mean just me. Well, not in the whole company, but I head up the IT department and we are in a satellite office, and today I am the only occupant. It's January 2021, COVID pandemic currently at its second peak and we are 'Tier 4 - Stay at Home'. Much of the department are either home working or furloughed. I have a small team onsite at the main office for warehouse support and then me, alone in an office meant for twenty people. I'm surrounded by Perspex, and still putting on my mask if I need to get up for the bathroom, or a coffee, despite having seen not a single soul for at least the last six Mondays I've been in the office.

At least it's only Mondays; I used to do this every day! Okay pre-pandemic there would have been more company, but it was still the same daily grind. Circumstances brought about predominately by a new C-Suite Transformation Officer, appointed above me, had made it a miserable last six months. Luckily, no sooner had this nightmare begun, a credibility-shaking announcement of pregnancy at least offered the reprieve of imminent maternity leave. This coincided almost exactly with the first national lockdown, so as well as the break from my new red-pen-wielding boss, I also had the advantage of working from home. Perhaps this COVID thing wasn't so bad as it seemed.

But it was bad. It was obviously bad in the most meaningful ways. People dying, families separated, the NHS at risk of gridlock, the economy on its knees. These were the important things, the scary statistics, the uncertain future, but it was bad in other ways too. Much less meaningful; nationally, globally, but meaningful to me...

So, a little more information. At time of writing, I work for a high street retailer operating in the UK. Bricks & mortar, as well as online, with an international franchise business and a fully owned Spanish retail chain. Somewhere under the corporate umbrella there is also a manufacturing business and a property business. This is a privately owned company, led by a born-again Christian and his family. Unfortunately, I am feeling somewhat less Christian myself at the moment regards work-life balance and lockdown has only highlighted to me that there must be more to life than the corporate slog!

Credit where credit is due, this company has been built from the ground up. The owner did not come from money; has a self-confessed lack of educational qualifications thwarted by dyslexia, but clearly had a powerful drive to succeed. I saw him interviewed once for a television program, Facing the Canon, and when speaking about his epiphany he did suggest he was not the nicest of persons before he found God. I don't know which shocked me more, the fact he thought he was a good person now, or the thought he may once have been worse!

Joking aside - and I appreciate this year has brought previously unseen challenges - the full store estate closed for months on end, sales and profits wiped out even with the unprecedented increase in online demand. However, at a time when the cascade from the senior team could have been more motivational, more rallying, unfortunately it seemed at times the only emotions cascaded seemed to be the stress, fear, and threat of the collapse of the business should we not all work harder, faster, longer.

There have been positives. The company topped-up the government furlough payments to 100% of salary for large parts of the lockdown period. Investments have been made in safety measures for those still working in the offices or warehouses. There have been various welfare communications and company updates but, as usual, the whole approach through this process has been somewhat bipolar for those on the coalface.

For those identified as critical to the ongoing operation of the business (me included) it has arguably been the toughest of times. Not because the work was tough - although it clearly was - but because it could often be accompanied by daily beastings. Real hairdryer moments. Accusations that nobody cared about the business's survival; pressure to attend the office even though government advice was 'work from home where you can'; accusations of incompetence in every area. Embarrassing outburst in meetings with many of your peers. And on the odd occasion that any positivity or praise was given, cynically, I would suggest, only when prompted, it would be palpably insincere. You cannot expect anyone to be content with limp praise when the previous day they had been treated with such public contempt.

The saddest part is this was not wholly unexpected behaviour. Possibly exaggerated by the extreme trading conditions but it was predictable. Almost expected. It served little purpose but to demotivate an already battered management team. We joked about it. While the meetings were in progress and today's victim was being lambasted, we might send each other messages on Teams to lighten the mood 'Yikes! Your turn today mate! Good luck' or such like. You had to make light of it. If you took it too seriously, you'd never sleep at night!

Even the positive moves that had been made backfired at times like these. We were having to put up with this behaviour for no reward at all. Even the guarantee of our salary was no improvement on furlough as that was being topped up to 100% anyway.

I tell a lie. There was a reward, three days additional annual leave! However, due to the excessive work demands of delivering major projects in extreme timelines to try and bolster opportunities, there was no time to actually book any holiday. It's now January, another lockdown is in place, and I have nine weeks left of the holiday year in which to try and book off three weeks of leave. Company policy does not allow for it to be carried forward of course...

I digress... this book isn't about my employment. I seek neither sympathy or redress and they are only my opinions. I am sure others feel very differently but this is how I was feeling at the time. Possibly it is an opinion tainted or exaggerated by my failing enthusiasm following the appointment of the CTO. I mention the above only to set the scene as to where my head has been, and why I am even writing this in the first place.

We are now in full lockdown again. This will be my last day in the office for a while as even the business leadership instruction this time is to stay at home. But even that prospect no longer lightens my mood. The first lockdown was a revelation. We can work remotely. Technically it all held together and for many people it was possible to be equally productive from the home office. I personally found great benefit in not having to spend three hours a day driving. A lie in and I'm still on the laptop doing emails earlier than if I was commuting. Win-win for me and the company surely? Despite the positives I anticipate this second lockdown will be as similarly a bruising experience as before. I am too old to be managed by stick, I need more than a carrot to motivate me these days.

But what to do instead? Job hopping is not really for me and the climate in retail right now is unsettled to say the least. I know what to do, I'll write a book. But what about? Well actually I've tried this before…

When I was seventeen, untainted by the world of employment, I had ambitions to be a writer. This ambition subsided as life took over, but it never went away. So now I am looking for a new release, a hobby, a distraction from the real world, I have had this little idea to write my biography and wrap it around my first attempt at a book, a story I wrote in my late teens.

Along the way I plan to analyse what was in my head at the time and, with hindsight, also how it may relate to the man I have become. An autobiography of an unknown person intertwined with an unedited first attempt at a novella by a teenage boy. Sounds like a bestseller to me.

You've already started reading the biography part I guess, so, now I've set the scene, let me treat you to the first instalment of the fiction. It was the late eighties, I was a teenager, this is unabridged, I apologise in advance.

Murder at St Philip's

Richard Godfray, age 17+

CHAPTER 1

It was a cold December morning. Snow lay thick on the ground and the skies threatened more would soon fall. The trees that lined the sides of the school driveway stood perfectly still, like white guards lining a street for a royal procession, with only the occasional clump of snow, falling softly from a drooping branch, to break the winter silence.

Wait! Cutting the peace of the day was a young boy running frantically across the courtyard in front of the main school building. One hand holding his schoolbooks close to his chest, the other clutching at the air as he tried desperately to stop himself from slipping head over heels in the snow. He could probably have walked faster but he was already late for class and could spare no time for rational thinking. He disappeared into the main building through a large ancient oak door and once again the grounds were peaceful.

9

How could anyone be late for school when they lived on the premises?

The main building that formed the 'St Philip's School for Boys' had been built some years ago for a purpose long since forgotten. The school, as an institution, had come by the premises in the later part of the nineteenth century courtesy of the will of an old eccentric. A man who could easily have been mistaken for a patient, rather than the proprietor, of the sanatorium the building had housed prior to the school's takeover.

Reminders of the building's history could still be found in many of the rooms, none more so than the library which had once been an operating theatre. The theatre lights still hung from the ceiling, the doors had little round hospital windows and the whole room was haunted by the atmosphere of the many gruesome operations that had taken place all those years ago when anaesthetic was in its earliest and most primitive stages.

Although the past was no secret, it was also not a subject for emphasis. A program of constant maintenance, restoration, extension, and expansion had, over the years, developed the building into a much more visually attractive property.

In the past, the work had been funded mainly by organised cash raising events and donations, but as the school began to develop a positive reputation it became possible to increase school fees to a level which provided ample funds to finance the most ambitious of projects.

A sports hall, sixth form block, science block and dining hall/theatre were just a few of the previous achievements, and the latest challenge had been the full restoration of a small church that had stood derelict within the grounds for almost two centuries.

It was from this church to the right of the main driveway that the sound of the school choir could be heard, drifting softly through the still morning air. The Christmas concert was fast approaching, and the rehearsals had been underway for some time. This session was coming to an end and the boys were finishing, as they always did at the end of a morning lesson, with a chorus of *Morning Has Broken*.

The church and the choir were a proud feature of the school, and a great deal of time and money had been spent developing them. All new boys to the school were invited to audition, though the standard was very high as the church had also taken to serving the local community and the boys were required to sing the regular Sunday service.

At present, the boys were all dressed in white robes with large, rolled collars, bar Jaymi, the lead choir boy. He stood at the front of the group in his boxer shorts and a T-shirt, his robe currently in the talented hands of Mrs Beavis.

Mrs Beavis sat to one side of the boys making the final alterations to Jaymi's costume. She was a typical dear old lady who lived locally and provided her services free of charge. It never even entered her head to curse when the bell for morning break sounded, causing her to jump and prick a finger on her needle.

'Right boys, go and get changed,' the Choir Master instructed as the ringing came to an end, 'Except Jaymi. Stay and try your robe again please.'

The rest of the boys shot off towards the changing room to re-dress in their uniforms before any more of break was wasted.

In the main school building Michael made his way from class to the top floor of the block. This area of the school was strictly out of bounds, so he crept quietly along each corridor checking ahead and behind as he went. Checking once more over his shoulder Michael entered one of the top floor rooms and closed the door quietly behind himself.

Once in the room he moved swiftly over to a small, dust covered, chest of drawers and removed from behind it a well-thumbed magazine. He placed it on a table to the right of his hiding place, and as his eyes scanned the familiar cover, he pulled a tissue from his blazer pocket and placed it beside the magazine.

Michael was already excited at the thought of what was to come, and hurriedly undid his trousers and let them drop to his ankles. He pulled his underpants down to his knees and with one hand, set firmly in plaster cast, he flicked through the pages of the magazine, and with the other he began to masturbate.

The choir had just finished changing. A few of the boys waited as Jaymi tied his shoes and put on his jumper.

'We've got to meet Mike out front,' Jaymi informed the others.

'Okay, but I want to go to the tuck shop before it shuts,' Ben, a rather plump boy, replied.

They all piled out of the changing room together, handed in their robes, then made their way out of the church.

Michael pulled up his pants and trousers, shut the magazine and placed the soggy tissue into his pocket. He replaced the magazine behind the drawers and left the room, checking first to see that nobody was coming. He walked briskly down the corridor towards the stairs, freezing momentarily as he heard footsteps approaching.

After diving into one of the rooms to hide, he heard the footsteps pass the door and he peeked out to see who was passing.

When the coast was clear he continued down the corridor and managed to get back downstairs without anyone noticing where he had come from.

He stopped at the toilets to get rid of the tissue which had begun to dampen the inside of his trouser pocket and used the toilet while he was there.

Jaymi was waiting for his friend outside the main entrance and started to walk over as he saw Michael coming out of the door.

'Where were you?' Jaymi asked.

'Taking a leak. Where's Ben and the others?'

'They went to get some food.'

The two of them walked off in the direction of the tuck shop in search of their friends.

'How was choir practice?'

'Not too bad,' Jaymi said with a smile on his face. 'Better than your Latin I should think.'

One of the main advantages of being a choir member was the necessity to miss certain lessons in order to practice. A fact Jaymi liked to remind Michael of whenever possible.

At thirteen, Michael was one of the oldest boys in their year and puberty had taken a firm hold of his body. He had been the first of their group, and probably their year, to masturbate. This Jaymi suspected through late night conversations in the dormitories and realised one sleepless night as he silently watched Michael's duvet bob up and down in rhythm with the soft panting of the boy below.

Michael's muscles were also developing, broadening his frame, and in the last six months he had outgrown all of his peers. His face too was losing its chubby boyishness and, if you looked closely, you could see the beginnings of a downy moustache, more obvious due to his dark colouring. Not to mention the fine brow of pubic hair, too short yet to be curly, which topped his maturing groin and was a feature he proudly boasted of to all his friends.

With all this physical maturity however, there had to come another change. Michael's voice was breaking, thus rendering him unsuitable for the highly esteemed school choir.

Jaymi was the complete opposite of Michael. He was one of the youngest and smallest boys in the year, and although he had recently discovered the full delights of self-exploration, his body was otherwise seemingly prepubescent. A fact the others often teased him over. His blonde hair and cute face added to his innocence, and his angelic voice had resulted in him being lead choir boy since year seven. He took comfort in this achievement and retorted to his friends that his body would develop, but they would never lead the choir. His position was quite envied.

'Anything is better than my Latin,' Michael answered. 'That bitch Miss Parks put me in detention again because I couldn't...'

Michael broke off in mid-sentence.

There was an almighty crash and the sound of breaking glass.

Michael, Jaymi and everyone else in the schoolyard turned in the direction of the noise and found themselves looking up at one of the top floor windows. Glass was still falling from the edges of the window frame and lower down their eyes caught sight of a body as it slammed on to the roof of the school minibus parked below.

Everyone was silent as they watched. Some of the boys turned away, some moved closer. The staff on break duty ran over to where the body lay and Miss Parks leapt up first onto the bonnet, then onto the roof of the minibus.

Michael gasped in amazement. Not only had he just seen a body fall from a window, but he had also witnessed a teacher he had little respect for go rushing to the rescue and begin administering first aid.

'Did you just see Miss Parks?' Michael asked, but before Jaymi could speak another teacher's voice was piercing the air.

'Can somebody fetch the headmaster and tell him to phone for an ambulance.'

A boy near to the school ran off on the errand. When he reached the headmaster's office, he paused for breath then rushed out his sentence as quickly as he could.

'Get the Head and tell him to phone an ambulance. There's been an accident.'

The secretary picked up the phone and called the emergency services. As she waited for the call to go through, she looked up at the boy in front of her.

'What's happened?'

'Somebody fell out of a window,' he explained. 'Mr Jones sent me to get the headmaster.'

'He's not here,' she replied then broke off to speak into the phone.

The Headmaster, Mr Price, appeared in the entrance hall as Julie, his secretary, finished the call.

'What is going on?' he inquired. 'I heard a commotion outside. What has happened?'

Andrew told Mr Price all he had told Julie then followed him as he rushed outside to the scene.

ANALYSIS 1

So, as I mentioned earlier, I am going to analyse each section and explain the biographical references and perhaps even the foretelling of future events through the eyes of hindsight. I may have only been seventeen when I began this story, but I really feel there are references in it that relate to many of the events that have subsequently shaped my life.

I am writing this in 'real-time' so to speak. The preface starts in January 2021, and it is still January as I write this first dissection of chapter one. It has been well over two decades since I even browsed the original manuscript and I have decided not to read the whole thing in full. Instead, I will read just the section presented and analyse it in isolation. I expect this will lead to a less than chronological biography, with the need to dip in and out and revisit periods of time in further depth at a later stage but let's see how it goes. An adventure down memory lane for me, an uncertain journey for you.

The story starts in the grounds of a rather grand secondary school. On reading back I am not sure I have yet captured quite how grand. My writing technique is very visual, I see everything in my head before it is transferred to the page, the tricky part is the transfer process. Even more difficult when based on actual events as when I read the words I am immediately transported to these places, and I suspect my prose does not quite evoke the same image in a reader's mind. All the same, this is a real place. Kent School, Hostert, West Germany. Well, it was West Germany at the time.

My father was a military man, a Royal Air Force lifer. His RAF career topped and tailed only by an apprenticeship at the Harland & Wolff shipyard in Belfast, and a final run into retirement as a civilian heating engineer on the same RAF base he retired from. Brize Norton, Oxfordshire, no more than five miles away from where I am writing this sentence. But for the moment we are back in Germany.

We moved to Germany just after I turned nine years old. It was the first of my father's postings I can remember, although this was the third move since I had been born during one of his previous tours in Malta. A chubby baby with peroxide blonde hair, I believe I was somewhat of a novelty for my parents' Maltese friends and acquaintances, presumably for the hair colour, as I've been back to Malta subsequently and chubbiness seems somewhat less uncommon.

The move to Germany was a big event in my young life but one I faced with excitement rather than fear or annoyance. Being an Air Force child of the seventies and eighties still meant regular moves, something that would diminish over time as cutbacks led to the closure of many camps around the world. I never feared a move, I always found it reasonably easy to make friends, but the moves could be annoying. Leaving friends behind was hard, although if you stayed, they would inevitably leave you behind as we moved in that military circle. The worst was at sixteen, but I'll come back to that.

Being only nine when we moved, big school, Kent school, was still two years away for me. In the intervening period I would first attend Merlin Primary, initially a bus journey away from our flat in Bauxhof, Erkelenz, but within six months we were living on the RAF base in Wildenrath, and Merlin school was just across the road from our new home. Number 6 Harrier Way if I recall correctly.

I have such fond memories of my whole time in Germany. The three and a half years we spent there were full of adventures and new experiences for me. A much nicer, safer environment than we had come from near West Drayton. Free to wander much further than you would allow any nine-year-old today. Playing on a frozen lake in Erkelenz, scrambling for safety at the sound of cracking ice and laughing hysterically once safely back on the shore. Or later, on camp, walking down abandoned railway tracks, or sneaking through holes in the camp fence and scrumping for apples in the local town. Or pinching corn cobs from a farmer's field and feeding them to deer through the fence of their enclosure. And always a whole new set of friends, all now lost but never forgotten. Adventures and events that shaped me in ways that still resonate today.

Not least was the move up to Kent school. It was such an impressive building. A complex of buildings really. The main school building was a four storey H-shaped affair with grand entrance doors. A separate science block, lunch block, sports block. An extension at the rear of the main building linked by a glass corridor. A boarding house and a church on site. The church was derelict, but we were given a tour of it in one of our lessons and it would clearly have been an impressive place of worship in its day.

There were stories aplenty for an impressionable eleven-year-old. The top floor of the building, as in the story, was out of bounds, unused and obviously haunted. In places stairwells had been blocked off, the steps abruptly ending against blank walls or ceilings, the wandering spirits safely bricked up behind. On another floor there was a dark corridor. Pitch black dark, no bulbs or natural light other than from a small glass square in the double doors at each end. Impossible to pass through unless you ran from end to end to escape the clutching hands of hidden creatures within.

Then there were the tunnels. A rumoured matrix of them below the buildings used for secret journeys and escapes by the Nazi soldiers that had once occupied the property. The tunnels were also forbidden, many blocked off, officially on grounds of safety but we knew it was to protect the litter of decaying bones now at rest in their unofficial grave.

I believe the Nazi's did once occupy the school, commandeering it during the war as a military hospital. It had certainly been a hospital at some point, the library was testament to that. It must have been a psychiatric hospital as everyone knew someone, who knew someone, that when finding themselves alone in the library, had heard the echoes of past screams as long dead patients received lobotomies or electrocution therapy, without the use of anaesthetic.

I loved being at this school, what was not to love? I could easily now do some research, check the real history of the place, pick the bones from the myths but what would be the purpose? I'd rather not know the truth for fear of diluting my memories. Just googling the correct spelling of the place names has already enlightened me to the facts that the flats in Bauxhof have since been demolished, RAF Wildenrath was disbanded and is now a civilian cargo airport, again with much of the housing demolished. Kent school is abandoned, derelict and decaying, even more ghostly now, I would imagine. The passage of time, it seems, is devouring my past like Stephen King's *Langoliers*.

In my time at the school, and for many years before I imagine, the church was unused. Unusable in fact. For my fiction, however, poetic licence allows me to restore it to glory as an enabler for the inclusion of a school choir. I have always enjoyed choral music and the title of the story itself, the renaming of the school to St Philip's, came about due to the appearance of The St Philip's Boys Choir on both *Top of the Pops* and an episode of *Wogan* during the mid-eighties.

The song performed was *Sing Forever* and I liked it. I put in a special order for the album at the local 'Our Price Records' and over the years have followed their evolution through to Angel Voices and Libera. On reflection, I suppose it wasn't only the name of the choir that changed over those years as the shelf life of a choirboy is fairly limited. Perhaps, on reflection, I had been loyally following the choral equivalent of Trigger's broom.

If I analyse deeper, which I am increasingly doing as I pen these words, I believe my love of choral music began in Germany at the military primary school I first attended. Merlin Primary, named after one of the Rolls-Royce engines from the spitfire aircraft, held regular assemblies attended by the camp chaplain. Hymns aplenty!

A sister school, Griffon Primary, sat on the opposite side

of a shared sports field, a mirror image building also named after a Rolls-Royce engine. There was great rivalry between the schools, however, Merlin was the better, obviously.

I was an avid group participant in assembly and was also appointed lead choirboy for a Christmas concert that was to be staged. I assume this was the festive brainchild of the music teacher as I don't recall there being a school choir prior to this. I remember auditions and I remember being selected to sing the solo, front & centre of the stage. I also remember missing the whole concert due to sickness. My rose-tinted memory would have me believe an opportunity was missed here but a more niggling part of my brain can't help suggesting I feigned illness due to a crippling case of stage fright that came over me as the event drew closer.

I wasn't a shy child, nor did I really lack confidence, but I would have hated to embarrass myself and putting myself in a situation that could lead to that seemed unnecessary. Hopefully, I have changed somewhat, or this book may never see the light of day.

Now, what else of interest is there to mention from the first chapter? We meet the first few characters, and I should explain some of the naming logic I followed both then, and some further rules I will be following in the 'now' sections of this story. All the names used in the fiction are taken from real people who have been in my life, although I am a little hazy on the origins of a couple of them. I should also clearly state that my characters are in no way a reflection of the source subject. Of course, there are elements that make it through, traits, likenesses, but realistically every character will be an amalgamation of people and experiences from my life. This is all I had to draw on and at seventeen my gene pool of acquaintances was somewhat limited.

Mrs Beavis, Miss Parks, Mr Jones, and Mr Price were all teachers from the various secondary schools I have attended. I have gender reassigned a couple of them, as is my wont. My father's RAF career saw me pass through two primary schools and four secondary schools by age seventeen. The joys of being an air force child.

Julie was a secretary at the first company I ever worked for, Floridan Ltd. Initially a summer job as a warehouse boy. Julie was the only secretary I knew, there was a secretary in my story, Julie seemed a reasonable name to use. Ben I cannot recall. I am wracking my brains, but nothing is forthcoming. I describe him as overweight, but I can't remember a Ben from those times, of any size.

The main characters of Jaymi and Michael have slightly more substance. The name Michael is taken from my first nephew, born just as this story was evolving. Too new in the world to influence this character, I incorporated various memories from other sources. A dose of Eugene, a friend from Germany, a dash of Darren, a friend from the posting directly after the German years and others I am sure I will recall.

My second nephew, Michael's brother, is coincidentally called Jamie but he would not arrive until after this story was all but complete. Fictional Jaymi was in fact no-one I knew, he was one of the boys from the real St Philip's Choir, hence the spelling of the name. Jaymi Bandtock was indeed one of the lead vocalists from the period I discovered the choir, it seemed fitting there should be a reference to him in the story. The character traits described in the fiction were predominantly taken from myself. I was that young, blonde, aspiring choirboy once.

For the biographical sections I have decided only to namecheck those that have brought positivity to my life in some way. Other people will be discussed, as in the preface, but I will not mention the names of anyone for whom I lack respect, anyone who bullied, or worse. I know already a truly horrific real-life murder will feature along with another more accidental death. The people responsible will gain no recognition here, they shall remain anonymous gender pronouns.

I think the only other thing that stands out from the first chapter would be the references to puberty and masturbation. I was seventeen, it was my specialist subject back then, what else was I going to write about? Seriously though, Michael's little fumble does become relevant later in the story.

So, there we are, the first scenes set, and the inner workings of my seventeen-year-old mind analysed. The school setting and the choral elements that start the story dissected and traced back to their origins. Let us read on…

CHAPTER 2

John Coles and his son Martin sat no more than ten yards apart on the bank of the river. They had been fishing there for the best part of two hours and the keep net was as empty as it had been on arrival. In fact, it had never been much fuller since it was purchased some years before.

John never did have much luck fishing. He remembered when he had been in his teens and gone fishing five or six times without a single bite. His technique had improved little, and it now appeared Martin had inherited his lack of talent.

As John sat shivering, he thought to himself, and concluded that he was mad to have even entertained the idea of going fishing on his day off. It was the middle of winter, the snow was inches deep and although he longed to, he never enjoyed the pastime.

John looked over at Martin and smiled at the irony of the situation. It was a school day. The reason Martin sat cold and damp in the snow, his breath visible as it passed through chapped lips, was the closure of his school for the day due to a heating failure. It had been decided the classrooms were too cold, and the children could not be expected to work in the conditions. Martin made eye contact with his father and took his chances.

'Can we go and play pool instead?' he almost begged.

'I thought you were never going to ask,' Coles said. 'You'll have to help me up though, I think my arse has frozen to the chair.'

They hurriedly gathered their tackle and unceremoniously dumped it into the boot of the car. The heater was turned to full, and they headed for home.

'What time does the pool club open?'

'It opened at nine I think,' Martin replied, 'but let's grab a shower first. I'm numb.'

'It's a deal!' Coles nodded. He could do with a shower as he was feeling less than manly himself.

John washed first, bringing himself back to a more reasonable temperature and a more acceptable size. Whilst Martin showered, he went downstairs to make coffee. As he passed the telephone table in the hall, he knocked over a picture of his wife and daughter together on the beach. It had been taken when she was pregnant with Martin, two years before the crash.

Mary, his wife, had been bringing Sarah home from playschool as usual when for some reason she had lost control of the car. It had veered off the road, through a hedge and over the edge of a short drop before coming to rest on its roof. A witness had rushed to help but was thrown to the ground as the car exploded into flames.

When the fire service had finally cut through the twisted metal, they had found Mary and Sarah's charred bodies still strapped into their seats. John had been told their deaths were instantaneous but had never believed it. That was what they told everyone. John knew this, he was a policeman, he had told the same lie himself hoping it would bring a little comfort to a grieving parent.

The only comfort John could seek from the whole disaster was that fate had kept Martin from the car that day. Mary had been having coffee at a friend's house and had lost track of time. When she realised it was almost time for her to collect Sarah from school, her friend had offered to hold on to Martin while she went to save her the time of putting him in and out of his baby seat. John often thanked God for this small mercy, but cursed him just as often for his loss.

The sound of the telephone interrupted John's thoughts.

'701643, John Coles speaking.'

'Where? Okay. I'll meet you there in about fifteen, twenty minutes.'

'Damn!' John thought to himself. He moved to walk upstairs and tell Martin he had to go, then turned back to the table and picked up the pen and the pad that sat by the phone. He scribbled a note and left it where Martin would find it. He knew his son would be as mad as hell when he read it, but Coles told himself that Martin would understand one day, and with that forced belief he grabbed his coat and was gone.

Martin heard the car starting and jumped out of the shower.

'Dad?' he shouted towards the door.

27

He wrapped a towel around his waist and ran downstairs.

'Dad?'

As he reached the bottom of the stairs, he saw the note on the table. He picked it up and read it.

> *Martin,*
> *Sorry. Had to go to work. I'll*
> *have another day off soon and*
> *we can do whatever you like.*
> *Try and understand. Sorry.*
> *Love Dad.*

But Martin did not understand. He screwed up the note and threw it across the hall. He kicked the wall then cried out in pain. He sat down on the bottom stair and held his foot. Tears were in his eyes, the note more the cause than the pain in his toes.

Martin and his father were close because of circumstance, but at eleven years of age he was now wondering if he had taken his mother's place as the policeman's wife. The phone would ring, John would excuse himself, and Martin would not see his father for the rest of the day. Only recently had Martin been allowed to stay home alone. Previously he had been left with friends, sometimes strangers and on more than one occasion at the police station crèche. He could not tell his dad how much it hurt. The silent treatment would give a sign but John would promise to make it up to him and so it went on.

Martin dried his eyes and went upstairs. He took some money from his father's dressing table and decided he would treat himself to some sweets and a video. His father owed him that much at least.

John's car slid to a halt on the icy gravel of the teachers parking area at St Philip's, just yards away from the scene of the incident. A young constable was on hand to greet him.

'Inspector Coles?'

'Indeed,' Coles acknowledged. 'What's the gist here then?'

'School caretaker took a tumble from a top floor window sir. Quite a mess.'

'I'm sure it is,' Coles agreed, looking around the yard as he spoke. 'Is Bradey here?'

'Over with the body sir. Just behind the minibus.'

'Better take a look then,' he sighed, as he moved away from his car.

Hundreds of eyes peered from windows everywhere as they walked to the minibus.

'Let's start by saying nobody is to enter or leave the premises without permission, and I want the room he fell from sealed off.' Coles ordered with certain authority.

'Already done sir,' Bradey informed.

'You must be a mind reader Bradey.'

'Well, I always did like a short story,' he retorted. 'Besides, we thought you weren't coming,' he added as he pretended to look at the time.

'Careful! This was my day off. I don't need you to put me in a bad mood.'

Coles lifted the blood-stained sheet that covered the dead man's body. He grimaced and looked away.

'The headmaster's just over there if you would like to have a word sir,' Bradey offered as an excuse for Coles to leave the scene. 'Mr Price it is.'

Coles walked over to the man Bradey had pointed out.

'Mr Price?' Coles asked to attract his attention.

'Yes?' Price returned. His eyes wide with an expression that clearly asked, *Who the hell are you?* An expression which did not fade until Coles had produced his identification.

'There's a few things I'm going to need to know. I wonder if you could help me?' Coles was polite and no more.

'I'll try my best. What was it you were thinking of?'

'I'll need statements from anyone who saw the man fall.'

'McWinney. Alan McWinney was his name,' Price interrupted.

'Right! I'll need statements from anyone who saw Mr McWinney fall, and I'd like to know where everyone was when the incident occurred. Can you arrange that?' Coles' opinion of the man before him was forming fast, and it was less than flattering.

'I can give you a list of pupils who attended any clubs, bar those, you'll have to ask them yourself. It was a break. The children are quite free to occupy much of the grounds,' Price informed, seemingly oblivious to his own manner.

'In that case is there a hall where we can set up an interview room?'

'This is a school, obviously there is a hall,' Price snapped. 'I'll get you a list of all staff and pupils and arrange for them to come down in classes.'

'Thank you,' Coles said with no real meaning. 'May I also ask your general opinion of McWinney?'

'I think I could safely say he was one of our most disliked members of staff. He liked to cause trouble. He was due to leave at the end of the term.' Price obviously had no qualms

30

about speaking ill of the dead. 'Are you assuming foul play?'

'I assume nothing,' Coles replied. *'Other than you're a twat!'* he would have loved to add.

'I don't suppose this is going to avoid the press?' Price asked, worried about the consequences of bad publicity for the school.

'I shouldn't think we'll be able to avoid that I'm afraid,' Coles smiled inside. He thanked Price for his time and walked away, calling for Bradey's attention as he did so.

'Come on Bradey. I want to take a look at the room he fell from,' Coles explained as he walked off towards the main entrance.

'Coming master,' Bradey mumbled as he ran carefully through the snow to catch up.

ANALYSIS 2

I have known a few Martins. Mary and Sarah were my grandmothers, neither of which I met, and John is almost all of the older men in my family it would appear. It seems in Ireland, in my family at least, they like to call you John regardless of your actual christened name. I won't keep explaining the names for fear of it becoming a bit tedious, going forward I shall only highlight one should I feel it particularly relevant.

You may expect the John and Martin relationship is going to reflect my own relationship with my father. I thought it would too, but I am not finding it there yet. We have been fishing together, although my dad actually enjoyed fishing and was good at it. I found the whole experience extremely dull. I went again with a teenage friend and the empty keep net was taken from that experience. A waste of too many hours on the banks of the Thames in Abingdon with Simon. I'm sure he'll crop up again.

I think before engaging in this deeper analysis of my life I would have said - in fact have said - that my relationship with my father was poor. I would struggle to remember any standout events or interactions from my childhood and had convinced myself we were just different people with nothing in common. Not a problem, no great angst between us, but no real bond either. I now have no idea how I came to this conclusion, maybe it just takes the passage of time to realise, maybe there was an event that muddied the memories. Yes, maybe that's it.

I can certainly conjure up memories. The fishing trips to a section of the Thames at the bottom of one of my father's friends' garden, not too far from Heathrow but a cottage setting that could have been deep in any countryside. Numerous childhood holidays to Cornwall, captured in hundreds of slides rather than photographs, as was the trend in the seventies. Evenings replaying these memories, watching slide shows of hot summers on the beach with sandcastles and laughter. Childhood holidays were always sunny right? Even in Cornwall.

I remember going to work with my father one day, on to the RAF base at West Drayton. It was probably his day off, or certainly after his shift had ended as I am sure the RAF didn't do bring your kids to work days. A large marquee was being erected for some social event or open day and I recall being launched into the air and landing on the roof section before scrambling to grab a guide rope and pass it down before jumping back down into my father's catch.

There are now so many things coming back to me. An unfortunate incident with a Christmas tree. I set it on fire early one morning with my dad's lighter and had to wake him up to rush downstairs in his underwear and grab the well ablaze tinsel tower and launch it into the garden. And more holiday adventures when we were living in Germany. Road trips to Holland and Switzerland, theme park visits, air shows, golf, another work visit to his squadron open day and close contact with the RADAR and bloodhound missiles he worked on.

So, the memories are there, and my father was present in my childhood with my recollection doing him a disservice over the years. In fact, he wasn't a father at all, he was a proper Dad to me and to my sisters, and a provider to the whole family.

I should clarify, he still is. Both of my parents are still with us, tipping eighty now, and my dads' character is as strong as ever. He is an intellectual man, arguably underachieving. He stopped one rank short of the ceiling of non-commissioned ranks in the RAF, turning down the opportunity to become a warrant officer, probably through contempt for his superiors. Perhaps he had reached the same tipping point I have in my own career.

I have also realised I am very much my father's son, characteristics I now accept and appreciate, and if I continue to grow into the man he has become I will have no complaints.

So, unlike Martin, I was not brought up by a single father, with my mother and only sister killed in a tragic car accident. We were a pretty standard military family. Dad, Mum, me and two older sisters, all still alive and kicking. I believe the reason for the family tragedy and the single parenthood, other than to pad out the pages, was to facilitate some tension and a reason for Martin to feature later in the story. I can think of a couple of reasons I may have chosen a car crash as the method.

My uncle Tony and a friend from my sixth-form math class, who's name I am struggling to recall, both died in car crashes around this time of my life. I don't know the detail of my friend's death; I was no longer taking that math class when it happened, and we were not acquainted outside of school. Uncle Tony's crash happened one day while drink-driving back from Scrabo Golf Club, Newtownards.

Initially he was reported missing by my aunt, although they were separated at that time, and his wrecked car was discovered a day or two later off the side of a steep part of the road. His body had been thrown from the car as he had not been wearing a seatbelt. I don't believe I am speaking out of turn when I say although accidental, his clear recklessness of both drink-driving and not wearing a seatbelt may have stemmed from a recent diagnosis of asbestosis. Without researching the exact dates, I couldn't say for sure which, if either, influenced my fiction but it seems logical that one or the other did.

With regards to the crime theme of the story *(sorry for the spoiler if you thought he jumped)*, I think that was inevitable. I was a child of the seventies and eighties and my TV diet, once I had moved on from *Trumpton* and *The Flumps*, featured all the detective classics. *Hawaii Five-O*, *Columbo*, *The Streets of San Francisco*, *Kojak*, *Heart to Heart*, *Poirot*, *Marple*, with more than the odd dose of *Murder, She Wrote* along the way.

Well, maybe not inevitable, it could have been a horror, which was my other love as a teen, but I was now living in Oxfordshire and *Inspector Morse* was prime time viewing so it kind of made sense.

Joking aside, real life crime was also sparking my interest at this time. When considering future options at secondary school, along with which subjects to study in sixth form, I had considered studying law at university. This plan, a bit of a stretch to call it a plan if I'm honest, went out the window due to another RAF posting of my father's which I will return to in due course.

One of the real-life crimes that caught my attention had been the murder of fourteen-year-old newspaper boy Stuart Gough in January 1988. I realise we have just passed the thirty-three-year anniversary of his death as I write this, and thirty-three seems to be a recurring lucky number for me. Luck seems an inappropriate word for these few paragraphs though.

While digging through my scribblings and printed manuscripts of the original St Philip's story I also came across a newspaper cutting from the time of this murder. I had forgotten I kept it but reading it back it did not feel thirty-three years had passed.

Stuart had been abducted on his paper round early in the morning of 17th January, his partially clothed body found under a pile of leaves two weeks later, sexually abused and bludgeoned to death with a rock.

The perpetrator, who as previously stated I will not name for fear of giving him any further exposure for his horrific crime, was arrested quickly. He had a string of previous convictions for sexual assault, and it is believed he may have had as many as twenty-eight other victims before his sickening needs escalated to the murder of Stuart. I read now, with some minor satisfaction, he has subsequently been handed a whole life tariff which will see him die in jail.

If this story is ever published and should any of Stuart's family come to be reading it, I would like to say your beautiful boy has not been forgotten, even thirty-three years later by a complete stranger. He lived, and lives on, in your memories and mine.

The next question I raise for myself is why the drama of the falling body as my opening hook? Is it a hook in a book, or is a hook in a song, maybe I'm wrong? Maybe the Cat in the Hat knows? I digress for my own amusement.

'I was twelve going on thirteen the first time I saw a dead human being…'

Stephen King, The Body

I was a little older than Gordie Lachance when I saw my first dead human being. I had just turned fourteen and we were on our first proper foreign holiday to Spain. It seems odd to say as I was born in Malta and had already lived or travelled to several other countries, holidaying in Ireland, in Germany along the Moselle and Rhine on several occasions, as well as a caravanning adventure in Switzerland. But the holiday to Spain, Majorca in fact, felt like the first proper one as we were living in England at the time and we were going on an aeroplane, to a half-board hotel, on a proper package holiday.

I loved it! As well as my parents and sisters, my aunt and uncle Tony were there with my twin cousins. I was the youngest, a boy juxtaposed between childhood and maturity. A true adolescent, happily embracing the physical changes and the additional small freedoms my parents allowed me.

We spent days on the beach, my oldest sister burning her feet to painful blisters while I took an all-over golden tan on my slim toned body. I have a picture of myself in rather short red shorts, reclining on the sand, squinting in the sun but still posing at the camera. It's a great picture, I have been known to pop it up on Instagram for a #TBT every now and again. Let's just forget the reason my sister was burnt yet I was nicely tanned, was because ten minutes before the photo was taken my mother was embarrassingly rubbing sun cream into me like I was still five years old.

When not being smothered in factor fifty, I was allowed to roam a little. Walking the beach taking in the sights and sounds of the local traders trying to sell all sorts of trinkets. One in particular sticking in my mind was the calls of 'Melones, melones, melones…' of a fresh fruit seller.

Of an evening, before we settled for our nightly entertainment at the Pink Panther bar, I was allowed to wander through the gift shops. I had some money to burn but it was hard to find anything suitable. It seemed even the most innocuous object I picked up had either a penis concealed within, a plastic banana or cucumber for instance, or a penis that popped out upon a squeeze. I remember a cute plastic gorilla who became alarmingly endowed upon a squeeze of his stomach. After some searching, I bought a couple of penis-free keyrings to take home for some school friends.

Most of our evenings were spent at the aforementioned Pink Panther bar next to our hotel listing to Pepe playing keyboard and singing cover versions of well-known songs. My aunt was particularly fond of *To All the Girls I Loved Before*, although knowing my aunt I suspect she was fonder of

Pepe! She was the over-eager customer who bought a copy of the homemade album he was trying to sell at the end of each show.

I felt more mature on those evenings. I was staying up late in a bar, the conversations were more adult, and I really felt I was growing up. Unfortunately, when the evenings were over, I had to go back and sleep in my parents' room on a camp bed as they had only booked two rooms for the holiday and my sisters were sharing the other one.

It wasn't too bad, we weren't in the room that much, and the extra few minutes a teenage boy needed in the bathroom went by unmentioned if not unnoticed. Restless nights were also a common adolescent occurrence, something to do with a reset of the body's circadian rhythm I believe. I am not sure if it was the ticking body clock or just the warm Spanish night that woke me this particular evening, either way I wandered out on to the balcony for some air.

We were on a high floor, the 5th floor possibly. I am not sure what time it was but there were still people sitting at the tables by the pool bar, maybe just staff winding down after their shift? I seem to remember a dustcart emptying bins on the road but before I could take much more in, all hell let loose.

I could not say with certainty if it was from above or just below but directly in the column of our balcony a body was falling. It hit the ground hard on a terrace area just above the pool level and didn't move again. A couple of guys from the tables beside the pool jumped up and ran to assist, clambering up on to the terrace and over to the body directly below me. Quickly there were others gathered but it must have been obvious nothing could be done. A sheet was placed over the body before my parents joined me on the balcony, wondering what the commotion was.

The last thing I remember about the evening was a young woman walking back from the town centre, dropping to her knees screaming just outside the hotel, presumably having just been told someone from her group had lost their life. I am pretty sure we just went back to bed. It hasn't haunted me; I didn't require therapy. I am not that kind of person now and seemingly wasn't then either. I don't even recall telling my friends about it when I returned home with their keyrings.

Now, thirty-seven years later, even the power of the internet cannot surface me an article on this event, so I am unable to namecheck another lost life that lives on in my memory. I hope there is no offence caused that they made it into my writings, albeit to repeat their fatal fall.

Echoes of a Boy

CHAPTER 3

Jaymi, Michael, Carl and Andrew were in their dorm. Jaymi and Carl sat on either end of one of the beds, the gap between them forming the play area for their card game. A tape recorder rested against Jaymi's thigh, vibrating with the volume, and in front of Carl's knees was a pile of change and a can of deodorant.

Gambling was forbidden in the school but rarely reprimanded. Smoking, however, was a much more frowned upon crime, but nonetheless undertaken. Carl was just lighting his second since being sent back to the dorm shortly after the accident.

'I don't know why you smoke,' Andrew announced. 'Nobody thinks any more of you for doing it.'

'It makes him feel hard,' Michael mocked, from where he lay on his bed.

'There's a first time for everything,' Jaymi took over.

'Tell that to the girls who owe me favours,' Carl defended.

'In your dreams Carl, in your dreams.'

'That's grand coming from you. I heard you thought you had a pube until you pissed out of it.'

The others now laughed along with Carl.

'The old ones are the best,' Jaymi answered but he knew this round of insults was lost.

Although the oldest of the boys was barely thirteen, and all were in the teething stages of puberty, Jaymi's total lack of pubic hair was noted amongst his friends, and when the banter started, this was the weak spot they targeted. Jaymi bowed down in graceful embarrassment.

Carl shuffled the cards and began to deal. He had won most of the hands so far, as he always did, and had forced Jaymi to start betting with IOU's.

'Sure, you can afford to play with the big boys?' Carl had one last dig.

'Just deal!'

Every one of them had their unique point. Michael his premature development, Jaymi his voice, and Carl his ability to con you out of anything. He was known for being one of the tough guys in the year and had a natural flare for any kind of gambling. Smoking too seemed almost natural for him. Well, as natural as it can be when you are twelve.

Now if this dorm had been the casting office for an upcoming film, Andrew would have been auditioning for the role of a character called either 'Brains' or 'Eugene'. His thick rimmed spectacles enhanced this image, and he was certainly an 'A' student, but he deviated from the stereotypical due to his popularity. He was well liked amongst his peers despite his geek-like deviations from the so-called norm. Classical music being one, but this was easily quelled as there was only one tape recorder in the dorm, and luckily for the others it did not belong to him.

Andrew was standing at the far end of the dorm looking out of the window. The room was directly below the one McWinney had fallen from. McWinney's body had recently been removed but the minibus was still in the car park. A police constable was washing off the pool of blood that had gathered in the dent made by McWinney as he landed on the roof.

Andrew stood by the window for quite some time just watching the activity below before going to his bed and lying down with a book he had been reading.

Michael was sitting up on his bed writing a letter. He had wanted to get it finished before lunch, although lessons had been cancelled for the rest of the day so there was no hurry.

'Shit! I'm through with this. You've got to be cheating,' Jaymi cursed.

'Too bad! I guess you're not cut out to play with the big boys after all,' Carl smiled back. He loved to win.

'Hey Mike, what you doing over there? You're pretty quiet.'

'Writing a letter,' he candidly replied without looking up from the page.

'Not to the soldier from Abingdon?'

'Yeah!' Mike snapped back. This time he did look up. 'The one from Abingdon.'

'I take it he can read?' Jaymi teased.

'You can be a real prick sometimes Jaymi.'

Michael was through with this conversation. He turned back to his writing paper.

Michael did not have many friends outside of school, in fact he had had none until he met Richard. They had befriended each other in the last summer holidays and had spent most of the days kicking around doing something and nothing. When Mike had gone back to school he had started to write and whenever he went home for a weekend, or a term break Richard would come looking for him and they would head off to do the something and nothing they always did.

Richard was older than Mike by two years, but they were much closer in appearance. Similar builds and features had once caused a stranger to ask if they were brothers. Michael had taken a bit of stick about it when the others had found out, but all the boys were mocked about something or another. The truth was he felt more in place when he was with Richard than he did when he was at school.

Unlike most of the boys at the school, Michael's father was not a rich man. He was in the Royal Air Force. This itself had its perks, one of which was that they paid part of Michael's school fees. However, he did like the boarding school and that was where most of his friends were, especially Jaymi, who despite the teasing that went on between them, was still his best friend. Ideally, he would have liked it if Richard could have gone to the school, but never mind.

Mike had just finished the letter when Ben, the fifth boy in their dorm, came running through the doorway.

'Someone's coming!' he cried. It had been his turn for lookout.

Carl and Jaymi both grabbed for the cards and money and as they did so they knocked the tape machine off the bed and onto the floor. The music came to a stop and all that could be heard were the coins they had been gambling with rolling across the floor. Jaymi picked up the money as Carl stuffed his cigarettes and makeshift ashtray under the mattress.

In just a few moments they were both sitting calmly on the bed amidst a cloud of deodorant, dispensed to cover the smell of smoking. Carl was shuffling the cards and Jaymi was trying to get his tape recorder to work again. He shook it and something rattled inside.

'Shit! That's the second one I've broken since July.'

The door to the dorm opened once more and Coles and Bradey walked in.

'Morning lads,' Bradey said.

'Morning sir,' they replied in unison.

'Come to question us, have you?' Andrew asked.

'No. You will all get a chance to make a statement later. We just wondered if you could point us in the direction of the top floor, we seem to keep running out of stairs.'

'Going to inspect the scene of the crime, are you?' Andrew quizzed once more.

'If indeed there was a crime,' Coles corrected. 'Didn't catch your name.'

'Well, you wouldn't have unless you're psychic. Andrew it is, and I think you can assume there was a crime.'

'Oh! Why is that then?'

'Well, the alternative is suicide, which technically is a crime anyway, but we won't count that, and if you were going to kill yourself, I hardly think jumping out of a closed window backwards would be the favoured method.'

'Want to be a policeman do you son?' Bradey asked.

'Not exactly,' Andrew smiled. 'Criminal law was more what I had in mind.'

'Oh! I see.' Bradey was silenced.

'Could someone please just tell us how to get upstairs?' Coles asked impatiently. He hated smarmy little kids.

Carl gave the directions. Most of the stairs had been blocked off to the top floor because it was unsafe, so Coles did not feel quite so stupid when Carl explained that the way up was behind a door at the end of the corridor. A door which looked just like another room to anyone who did not know better.

Coles and Bradey turned to walk out of the door but before doing so Coles turned to Carl and said, 'I hope the person who sold you cigarettes realises it's against the law, besides, you might get a detention if you're caught.' With that they left.

'Damn!' Jaymi exclaimed as he jumped up from the bed and headed for the door, 'I've got a French detention.'

'Hang on a minute,' Michael mumbled as he licked a stamp then stuck it on his letter. 'Post this for me.'

Jaymi took the envelope and shot off down the corridor, walking only when a teacher came into sight. As he reached the letter box which served their floor, he saw that one of the sixth form students had just emptied it and was walking away with the sack.

'Take this one would you please?'

'Sorry!' The senior smiled back, 'You just missed the post.'

'Take the boy's letter Walton,' Mr Price said from somewhere behind Jaymi, then reached over Jaymi's head and took the letter himself.

Jaymi left the two of them to work it out and carried on towards his French class.

Mrs Baxter was sitting at her desk reading a book when Jaymi arrived. As he walked in, she put it down out of his sight.

'Yes? Jaymi,' she said.

'Detention Miss, I've got a detention.'

'You did have a detention, for which you are late, but in light of the circumstances I have pardoned you so you can recover from the obvious shock of having lost a member of staff.'

'What?'

'It's pardon Jaymi, not what. Never mind, just go back to your dorm and wait for lunch.'

Jaymi left the room and Mrs Baxter went back to reading her book, *The Happy Hooker* by Xaviera Hollander. It did little for her French, but it reminded her of what she missed most since her divorce.

ANALYSIS 3

I never went to boarding school myself, although it isn't un-common for forces children to do so. Kent school did have a boarding house although, like me, the vast majority of pu-pils were day students. My sister boarded briefly when we moved back from Germany. The posting had coincided with the last year of her schooling so my parents had agreed she could stay on in Germany to complete her exams when we return to the UK.

I have subsequently heard stories from her about this time. When I was at a similar point in my own education we were posted again, and I was absolutely not allowed to stay at my previous school. I suspect her time alone in Germany had something to do with my parents' decision on this. Thank you, Beverley!

I did, however, have some dorm-room experience that obviously filtered its way into my teenage writings. During the mid-eighties - I believe the year after the Majorca holiday

- there was a residential school trip to Kilvrough Manor in South Wales. I had never really taken part in many school trips. We weren't a family that could throw funds at a vanity skiing trip, my language skills were poor therefore I did not select French or indeed even German for my options, so any foreign school exchanges were not on the agenda either.

The trip to Kilvrough was a Geography field trip, presumably sensibly priced, so my parents allowed me to put my name on the list. I think it is safe to say I was a touch of a mummy's boy growing up, protected behind her apron from my two mean big sisters. I'm sure they speculated that I would be unable to cope away from the family for a week. They were wrong.

Although angelic in appearance and bashful on first meeting (even if I do say so myself) do not be fooled, I was no angel, then or now. Certainly not a demon either but perfectly confident, able to hold my own within my peer group. I may even go as far as to say I have a manipulative side to my nature.

Manipulative may be too strong a word as it has quite sinister connotations, I think my skills are more positive in nature. I feel I often have the ability to discreetly steer situations in the direction I would like, not necessarily for my own gain, just to create an outcome I think would be good, or funny, or in everyone's interest. A little controlling perhaps, but harmless, I hope! The secret is out now anyhow so I may well have compromised that superpower going forward.

The week in Kilvrough was great for me, I thrived with barely a thought for the family back home missing their sweet little boy. We went climbing, abseiling, potholing, cliff walking to see a blowhole in a rocky outcrop in the sea. We walked the Brecon Beacons, had an orienteering adventure after dark to find our way back to the manor house, waded in a river near an oxbow lake. There were fun and games back at the manor too and I seem to recall a barbeque and larking around in the grounds.

It was action packed and I took it all in my stride, but it wasn't for everyone. One of my friends on the trip, formerly believed to be a bit rough and tough, refused to climb and abseil. He had kept on a brave face all morning and allowed himself to be harnessed up in the safety gear, I'm sure with every intention of taking part, but when it came to his turn he completely froze and could not even attempt the climb. He also developed a crippling case of homesickness and was quiet and withdrawn for the remainder of the week.

I learnt a few things on that trip about perception versus reality, not judging people too harshly, and how proceeding confidently, even when a little scared or nervous yourself, cannot only cement your self-confidence but can also change your standing within a group.

I took this bull by the horns on the first evening when we were all directed towards the group showers before getting ready for bed. As we approached, towels and PJs in hand, it seemed everyone was slowing down. Chatting and walking slowly, then undressing even more slowly when in the shower room. The first boy into the shower kept his underwear on but nobody said anything, minds too occupied wondering if they should follow suit and do the same. I was one of the youngest in my year, and although it does not necessarily go hand in hand, I was also one of the least developed physically. Oh well, nothing ventured nothing gained, I dropped my underwear and strode off to the showers naked.

This set the precedent and the boy in pants was soon in the minority, although not alone. Joviality replaced the nervous atmosphere in the room and before long everyone was larking around and attempting to towel-whip exposed buttocks as pyjamas were hurriedly pulled up. On reflection, our varying degrees of physical development were minimal, and nobody was going to say anything or judge, pants on or off, as everyone was equally embarrassed at showering with their friends.

Following the showers and a bit of down-time, it was off to the dorms. It was a room of six, three sets of bunkbeds, and I had earlier claimed a top bunk. The evenings in the dorms were just more larking around. Chatting rubbish, dares, farting, giggling. One of the lads also had a camera with him and it had at least one picture on it of my mooning arse hanging off the top bunk. The fun continued until a teacher yelled and the lights were turned off. A little more whispering and eventually we all fell asleep.

These are the kind of events that shaped my writing in the St Philip's story. A collage of my limited experiences at that time. You've read a few of them already and you'll recognise more as we work our way through.

The next bit of fact within the fiction that stands out to me is the reference to the pen pal relationship Michael has with Richard. As with most of the fictional characters and events within my story, they are a medley of real-life people I have known and various experiences in my life to that point. For this part Michael and Richard are two very specific people from a milestone period in my life. However, on re-reading those few paragraphs I am taken aback how, on this occasion, rather than relay an anecdote I have instead transcribed a fiction that I wish had been the reality.

This period of my life stayed with me and resurfaced much later, which I will go into at some point, so with hindsight I am fully aware of how impactful it was but, until reading back this story, I had no idea it had clearly impacted me equally at the time.

The real-life Michael was Darren Hall, and the real-life Richard was me. At the time I was living in Abingdon, Oxfordshire and this move was directly after my time in Germany. Darren came into my life for a very short period of time, roughly six months towards the end of my time in Abingdon. For reasons I will go into when I return to this period of my life later, I made a concerted effort to get to know Darren. I wish to this day there had been more time.

I first noticed Darren during February half term. He was at boarding school, so our interactions were only during school holidays. As with mine, Darren's father was in the RAF, and they lived in the married quarters no more than five hundred yards from ours. He had gone to one of the local schools for a period of time, but he didn't seem to have any local friends as he was always wandering around alone. He caught my eye and I decided immediately I would get to know him. My manipulation skills kicked in.

Now as I am trying to put this down in words, I am conscious it may all sound a bit stalkerish. Maybe it was. I would keep a lookout from our front room window, which had a reasonably panoramic view of his house, past the swing park and up to the sports field where the RAF football teams would play regular matches. Very quickly I had an idea of his routine and I decided to attempt contact.

It was now the Easter holidays, 1986, and one of the first times we spoke was in the swing park. It was a rainy day, but I had seen him walk into the park entrance across the road from my house, so I put my coat on and headed over. Darren was sitting on the swings rocking slowly back and forth in the rain. He was wearing jeans and a speckled cream coloured jumper, covered by a blue cagoule. He had white socks on beneath black Adidas trainers, and against the weather wore a flat cap and grey fingerless gloves with a yellow stripe across the knuckles. I joined him on the swings, and we had our first conversation.

Unsurprisingly I bumped into Darren again a few more times before the Easter holidays were done and conversations progressed and the exchange of information that happens as new friendships build continued. We were two years apart in age, thirteen and fifteen. I was surprised at first, I thought we would have been the same age but as I said before, I was a late developer.

There would be another half-term and again we would learn more about each other. I could tell you where he was born, where he had lived, changes of schools, where he went to boarding school, the car his father drove. He had siblings, he had a dog, he liked art, he was very sporty. I was soaking up information like a sponge, but the friendship was cemented during the summer holidays.

For all the things I can remember, I am not quite sure how at the start of the summer holidays Darren seemed to have acquired a local girlfriend, Rebecca. She went to my secondary school, Fitzharrys, and I know Darren had gone there for a short period so presumably he knew her from then. Rebecca had a best friend called Maxime, so I started going out with her and we spent time together as a four-some. It's quite telling that I do not have the same recall for any information about Rebecca or Maxime, other than my sister's teasing that Maxime had very large feet for a teenage girl.

During the summer holidays we spent lots more time together, usually on the grassy area beside Darren's house kicking a ball against his garage wall. We watched a film on somebody's sofa, arms around our girlfriends, maybe even a snog but certainly nothing more. I remember listening to music in Darren's bedroom whilst lounging around on his bed, *A-ha* if I recall correctly, and on another evening, we went to a party at Rebecca's house. It must have been a lat-ish party as it was dark when we returned on our bikes, and I had been trusted by Darren's mother to bring him home safely as I was that much older.

I am not recalling this all from memory, although I mostly could. I have notes about Darren I wrote at the time and that I have kept all these years. I aspired to write from an early age, and I have lots of notes on events and ideas that could be shaped into stories. The newspaper clipping on Stuart Gough was another example. Even now I question if this obsessional behaviour with Darren was sweet or creepy. Either way I know it was very important to me.

I enjoyed that summer so much, it was a real adolescent coming of age period in my life. I was devastated when it horribly and abruptly ended due to another RAF posting for my father. By the end of the summer, I had moved away ready to start over at a new school. For the first time I pro-tested, well sulked at least. The tragedy of the whole move for me was that it was one of our shortest. We were to re-main in Oxfordshire, only fifteen miles up the road from

Abingdon but there was absolutely no persuading my parents that I could return for school or any other purpose.

I did ride my bike back over there one weekend and I actually spoke to Darren's sister, but he was not there. I wrote a letter too, but I have no idea if it arrived, if I even sent it to the correct house number, or if possibly they had moved away themselves by then. Either way there was no reply. There was no pen pal relationship as in the fiction, this was poetic license I guess, a reality I wish had happened. Darren was gone from my life. Not for forever, but for the longest of times.

CHAPTER 4

Coles and Bradey found their way upstairs and walked the short distance down the corridor to the room McWinney had fallen from. Bradey nodded to the constable on the door, and he stepped aside allowing them to enter.

Nothing in the room seemed to be out of place indicating a struggle, and apart from the layers of dust, and the broken window it could have been any other school room.

Detectives worked checking for fingerprints in the obvious places someone may have touched on entering the room, but as yet they had been unsuccessful.

'Right Bradey, let's search this place. If there's a clue here, I want to find it.'

'Won't the lads have already done that sir?'

'I don't care if bloody Sherlock Holmes has already done it. I want to look myself,' Coles replied with the sound of authority in his voice again, and this time Bradey did not answer with a joke. He knew his place.

For the next three quarters of an hour, they searched on, in, and under everything in the room and when they had double-checked the areas the other had searched, they stopped to compare notes.

'Find anything Bradey?' Coles asked hopefully.

'No! You sir?'

'Nothing but dust and mouse shit!' Coles said. 'I was hoping there would be footprints, but whoever was in here has wiped them away. Come on, let's see if we have better luck in McWinney's rooms.'

Coles was ready to leave when Cleaps, a man he knew well, walked in. Simon Cleaps was a pathologist. He had worked with Coles before on several occasions and knew what he was like.

'Solved this one yet, have we?' he asked.

'Well actually I was just going to ask your opinion, so we're pretty desperate.'

Coles always seemed to greet people with an insult but despite this he got on very well with most of his colleagues. Everyone knew he was a good policeman despite his attitude, and Coles, knowing the fact, liked to take liberties.

'Not much to report so far,' Cleaps said. 'All we have is a body with injuries to suggest the cause of death was a fall from a great height. Not much help I suppose?'

'Nothing else at all?'

'Well,' Cleaps added, 'he's got a cut on the back of his head which I'm not convinced was caused by hitting the minibus. That's why I'm up here. I want to take a few samples and see if what I think, is right.'

Coles smiled. Whenever a pathologist says 'Not much to report' you always know there is a little something they're keeping back!

Cleaps moved to the window and began to examine it. He took blood samples from the pieces of glass that were left in the window frame and sealed them in a specimen bag he had taken from his pocket. He then stood on the windowsill, with an officer holding his belt, and started to examine the top of the frame.

'What do you think may have caused the cut to the back of his head if it wasn't the fall?' Bradey asked.

'I think I've just found the answer to that question,' Cleaps said. 'Come and take a look at this.'

Coles and Bradey moved to the window and looked up to where Cleaps was pointing. On the inside edge of the window frame was a thin line of blood where McWinney had obviously cracked his head on the way through the glass.

'Great! So now we know he banged his head on the way through,' Bradey said. 'It hardly makes a difference to the poor man, does it?'

'Yes Bradey,' Coles said, 'but don't you see? It confirms what little Andrew said about jumping through the window backwards. I think we agree that would be pretty unlikely, and I'd say McWinney must have been about 5'8' or 5'9' and the frame is over six feet from the ground, so how could he have hit his head if he had merely fallen?'

'Oh, I see what you mean.' Bradey caught on. 'So, you think maybe someone picked him up and pushed him through?'

Cleaps joined the conversation.

'I think if someone had picked him up there would be more signs of a struggle. It's more likely someone shoulder charged him. Their momentum could have lifted him off his feet without too much trouble I would have thought.'

'So, are we looking for someone quite hefty?'

'Not really. I think you could rule out most of the juniors, but then again you'd be surprised the strength you can muster when someone pisses you off.'

Coles seemed much happier now. He had been certain the fall was suspicious, and now he had a little piece of evidence to reinforce his belief. There was nothing he hated more than a suicide. It was such a waste of life - not to mention the paperwork.

'Come on Bradey,' Coles said. 'I think we've got a murder to solve, but first, let's eat.'

The dinner bell had rung a few minutes ago and reminded Coles just how hungry he was. He had skipped breakfast to go fishing and besides, he could not work on an empty stomach. They bid farewell to Cleaps and left the room in search of the dinner hall.

Gerald leant with his back against the hot air blower in the toilets. He listened, his face twisted in sympathy and disgust, to his friend, Dominic, being violently sick for the third time in the last ten minutes.

Dominic had woken up shivering and with a fever. Gerald had told him to go and see the nurse, but he had insisted that he would be alright. Since then, he had been sick seven, maybe eight times and had lost more colour than Michael Jackson.

Gerald walked forward and pushed open the door of the cubical in which Dominic sat with his head bowed deep into the bowl.

'That's it! If you don't go to the nurse then I'm going to go and get her,' he said, more with worry than anger.

'Okay! I'm coming,' Dominic replied, then trailed off into another agonising retch.

When Dominic was able, they both left the toilets and headed for the sick bay. He was only sick once on the way and luckily that was into one of the sinks in the chemistry lab, so Gerald was able to poke most of the lumps down the plug hole with a stirring rod he found on the side. Hell, what are best friends for?

There were two other boys in the sick bay with the nurse when they arrived, seemingly suffering with the same problem as Dominic.

'Must be a spot of flu going around,' the nurse said. 'Not much else wrong with you. Just got a bit of a fever. I think you can sleep the night here though, just so I can keep an eye on you.'

The three of them groaned. Staying the night with the nurse meant no television, no smoking, no anything!

Gerald smiled.

'I'll go and get your stuff. Have fun!'

'Ha, Ha! Just don't forget my Walkman,' Dominic called after him.

School dinners were pretty much as Coles remembered them from his own childhood, but he was too hungry to care. Mr Price had asked him his opinion of them, and he had politely lied. Bradey had also complemented the meal, but his opinion seemed genuine. He had gone back for seconds and still finished ahead of Coles.

'Where are you off to next?' Price asked out of curiosity.

'Mr McWinney's rooms,' Bradey replied, as Coles had a mouthful of food.

'What are you hoping to find?' Mr Davies asked. Davies was the PE teacher and did not appear to be interested in any other way than keeping the conversation alive, which had been lacking at their table all through lunch.

'Anything. I'm not really sure,' Bradey continued. 'Clues I suppose.'

Price asked them if they would like any more food. Coles replied with a quick 'No!' as soon as the sentence was complete. Bradey considered, then also declined on catching a glance of the look Coles threw in his direction. They excused themselves from the table and left the hall.

ANALYSIS 4

On the face of it there is not a huge amount of newness in this chapter to dive into and reference back to my historical experiences. Bradey is not a character based in fact as far as I can recall. Every detective needs a sidekick and I think he was created for that purpose alone, maybe there is something later on that will spark a memory, but I don't want to read ahead. The process of reading each chapter in turn and then analysing it in isolation is achieving what I have set out to do. I have no idea if it is working for the layman reader but for me it is proving very cathartic.

That said, the lovely little description of Gerald poking Dominic's vomit chunks down the plughole in a show of true friendship did occur. It happened when I was at a sleepover with one of my Fitzharrys school friends, David. It was his birthday and we had partaken in a little too much teenage drinking. I was almost a year younger than David, and certainly no big drinker, however, I was fine, David was not.

We had been in a pub garden for most of the evening, just a small group of us that had been at school together. I had moved away already but I was allowed back for his birthday, hence the sleepover. It had been a fun evening of joking around, reminiscing and drinking. I think a couple of David's pints may have contained the odd vodka shot and he was happy but struggling by the time we headed back to his house.

David's father, who I am certain was called Brian, greeted us when we stumbled in through their back door, me trying to hold David up by the shoulders. He made the wise decision to leave us to it when he realised I was still compos mentis and in control. Another three steps into the house and David vomited into the kitchen sink. I was the friend pushing down the lumps and cleaning up before putting him to bed with a glass of water.

Another recollection, when toying with names for the minor characters, is the pathologist surname being an anagram of scalpel. Of course, it isn't, as I had to remove an 'L', which means it is nowhere near as clever as I had intended. I was also a great lover of school dinners for the record. All the little memories you form together to create fiction, I guess that's how it works for all writers.

In terms of the story, this chapter is serving to pre-position a couple of clues and characters so the ties back to my boyhood are minimal. As we progress through the biographical part of this exercise, I am also conscious that the best part of two thirds of my life has taken place after this story was completed. My intention is to still weave this through the fiction and my related experiences, with an expectation I will need to dart around through time as I try to make sense of it all. Until then I will digress in a slightly different direction.

I am fully aware I am no literary genius, nor was I a child prodigy who has since lost this ability. Where I have always had confidence, is in my ability to attempt any task. This has never changed, even now aged fifty I have the same outlook. During this most recent COVID lockdown period I have purchased a Novation Launchpad and am using Ableton Live Lite to create my own musical arrangements. I have no musical background, I can play no instruments, but I am perfectly confident I can Google the techniques and create something I like, for my own amusement and pleasure.

As a teenager I enjoyed reading, often believing I could have taken a story in a different direction - a better direction - so I decided I would write some stories of my own. I don't believe this was arrogance on my part, I just liked to try things for myself, and I really didn't believe anything was outside of my ability. Maybe that could be a definition of arrogance, I suppose.

Looking back now I realise some things certainly were outside of my ability. I noted previously that perhaps my descriptive writing was not detailed enough, falling short as many of these experiences were real to me. Therefore, I was filling in large sections of detail in my head that did not exist on the page. A few chapters in, I am also finding reading back large sections of speech utterly cringeworthy. I needed some creative writing lessons, quite possibly I still do!

What I lack in talent I make up for in technical detail, I like to think so at least. I don't mean the technicalities of policing or such, I am sure there are just as many flaws with that as with my English. I mean the technicalities of putting a manuscript together. I remember putting in time researching best practices for manuscript writing. Double line spacing, text justification, hyphenation, words per page, margins, etc... I armed myself with whatever knowledge I could find. I had been earning some money from my first job, and even managed to upgrade from an old typewriter with the very proud second-hand purchase of an Amstrad PCW 8512 word processor. All the gear, no idea - so to speak.

And there I would sit, crafting my stories. Murder at St Philip's was by far my most ambitious piece but there were other short stories, and the beginnings of ideas for other bigger reads. At some point life took over and working and paying the mortgage became more important but I am pleased to be back revisiting my creative past. I hope this idea of presenting the 'as was' manuscript, non-enhanced from when my seventeen-year-old self first began to commit it to paper, wrapped in hindsight and biographical analysis is something that will be of interest to readers. Publishers first though, I suppose.

With that in mind, I recall another tip from the how-to writing guides of the day. No need to wait until the manuscript is complete before divining for interest with literary agents. Apparently an equally acceptable approach is to submit a synopsis and sample chapters for appraisal. Impressed publicists will then fall over themselves offering large advances to secure the publication rights of the masterpiece. Well, something like that, maybe.

As we stand, I have now presented four chapters and provided the first insights into the source events that inspired my fictional creation. I have prefaced with my current mood and motivation for starting this venture and, subject to review, I am happy with how it is shaping up. I am still very uncertain it will be of interest to anyone else, however, I am willing to try.

I am writing this with a real-time narrative, today being 22nd February 2021 and Boris is currently on the television in the background laying out his irreversible roadmap out of lockdown. If literary success is to be my route out of the rat-race I need to get a move on to minimise the time I am going to have to spend back in the office. So, I will start my pitching process in the background and keep you all informed on progress. Clearly if you are reading this, I will have at some point had success but who knows what setbacks or embarrassment may come before then.

I am also a realist, if literary success does not arrive, I still have plan B, lottery success. If that happens I will vanity publish the whole thing regardless of merit and you may be unfortunate enough to stumble across it that way.

Echoes of a Boy

CHAPTER 5

Coles and Bradey walked across the schoolyard towards McWinney's quarters. The snow crunched under foot, and as Bradey walked, he tried to step in the foot holes left by the last person to walk that way since the fresh snow fall. Obviously one of the boys, as the footprints were several sizes smaller than his own.

'What the hell are you doing?' Coles asked as he looked back to see what was keeping Bradey.

'Nothing sir,' Bradey answered as he straightened up and trotted to catch up.

McWinney's rooms were down beside the gates of the school at the bottom of the drive. The door was guarded by one of the officers Coles had assigned to the task, and as they moved closer, they could see the second one arriving with two cups of coffee.

'Hard at work I see lads,' Coles said as he and Bradey arrived at the door.

'Without sugar isn't it sir?' the constable with the coffee replied as he offered one of the cups to Coles.

'Very quick, but you can keep it,' Coles said as he made his way through the door, beckoning Bradey to follow him.

The insides of the rooms were clean and well organised. The place was filled with all the latest equipment including satellite television, and even though McWinney never had to pay rent Coles imagined most of his wage packet was accounted for in direct debits to Curry's and other such outlets.

'Nice little place he had,' Bradey commented. 'I wonder what they'll do with all this stuff?' he added as he examined a talking remote control.

'Not my problem,' Coles said. 'Now let's see if we can find anything of real interest.'

Bradey started to look through the drawers and cupboards in the front room, while Coles went through to the bedroom.

They searched in silence for nearly an hour. Bradey found nothing out of the ordinary in the front room. There were records, letters, and drawers full of all kinds of things that people collect for no apparent reason, but nothing to suggest any motive for murder.

After exhausting his front room search, Bradey moved on to the kitchen, where he found only pots and pans and cutlery - and all the other things you expect to find in a kitchen. Not to mention a top of the range microwave and electric everything else of course.

Bradey was just beginning to get tired of searching when Coles called him through into the bedroom.

'Take a look at these,' Coles called, with an excited overtone in his voice.

Bradey rushed through the door to find Coles sitting on the end of the bed with a shoe box by his side. He was flicking through some photographs, and as Bradey moved closer he could see that the box was full of money.

The picture Coles was now looking at, was of Mr Price and another man walking along the local town High Street. Both Coles and Bradey recognised the public house in the background of the picture - it was well known by most people in the area - and from other recognisable features of the photo they could tell that it had been taken from an alleyway on the opposite side of the street.

'Now why would McWinney have pictures of Price in a box full of money?' Coles asked himself out loud.

'Blackmail?' Bradey asked in reply.

'Could be,' Coles agreed. 'I want you to take this money back to the station, and when you're there get the film in that camera developed,' Coles said, pointing to the dressing table on top of which sat a camera.

'What about the photos?' Bradey asked.

'Take them as well, but we'll need them again tomorrow,' Coles said as he stood up and walked towards the door. 'I'm going to spend what's left of the afternoon in the hall interviewing, so I'll see you tomorrow at the station, eight o'clock sharp!'

Coles left Bradey to tidy up the mess they had both made while searching and made his way back over to the main building. He asked a wandering student for directions, then found his way to the hall Price had organised for the mass interview room.

In the hall there were two rows of desks, one down each side of the room. A police officer stood at the entrance and directed people who had been outside and seen the fall to one area of desks and people who were elsewhere at the time of the accident to another. Coles decided to go first to the 'elsewhere' section.

There were five police officers spread evenly along the length of the tables, each with a pupil sitting opposite them and a notepad on the desk in front. They all asked the same questions and noted down the answers each pupil gave them, along with their name and signature when the statement was complete.

Coles moved slowly along the line, before stopping by the side of a policewoman who had just started to question a new boy.

'Can I have your name please?' she began.

'Timothy Edwards,' came the nervous reply.

'Can you tell me where you were when the accident happened?'

'I was in the church,' Tim answered quietly. 'Auditioning for next year's choir.'

'I'll need the names of anyone who saw you there, and the names of as many others you can remember seeing.'

'Well, there was Mr Green, Mrs Beavis and Oliver Harper.'

The officer wrote down the three names Timothy had mentioned, then looked up at him again.

'Anybody else?'

'No,' he replied. 'Me and Oliver were the only two auditioning.'

Coles soon tired of listening to the same questions asked and answered time and time again and decide that nothing much could be achieved until the cross-referencing stage had begun. He moved across the hall to the other group of tables and took a seat. He motioned to the officer on the door for the next boy in line to be sent in, then picked up the pencil from the table and wrote his own name and the date at the top of the page. When he looked up, he saw a face he recognised.

'Hello again,' Coles greeted. 'We met upstairs. You were with Andrew, right?'

'Yes sir,' Michael replied.

'Well, I'll tell you what I will need to know, then you can reel it off all in one go while I write, that way it won't seem so much like twenty questions, okay?' Coles asked, then proceeded after receiving a positive nod from Michael.

'I'll need your full name, then where you were just before the accident, who you were with, where you were when the accident happened, what you saw and the names of as many people you can remember seeing with you when it happened, but only if you are sure they were there.'

Michael nodded once more, took a few breaths, then began to recall as much as he could - bar his trip to the heights of both the school and pleasure.

'I had just been ... Oh! Michael Bracher,' he corrected himself. 'I had just been in Latin. I left the class on my own and went down to meet my friend outside. I stopped to go to the toilet on the way. Jaymi Lowman, my friend, was already waiting for me when I got outside. We were going to the tuck shop to meet some other friends when we heard the glass break. I didn't actually see him come through the window, but I saw him land.' Michael paused for Coles to catch up.

'Go on,' Coles said when he had finished writing. 'You're doing great.'

'Miss Parks was there but I don't know if she saw me, but Jaymi did, and Andrew saw me. He was sent to get the headmaster. Andrew Morley that is, the one who was upstairs.'

Michael continued for a few minutes trying to remember the boys who had been outside, then left after Coles thanked him for his help.

Coles finished writing his notes on Michael, then tore off the page and put it to one side, face down of course. He headed the next page exactly as the first and called for the next boy in line to be sent over.

Coles spent the rest of the afternoon in the hall asking the same questions to what seemed like an endless queue of boys, and only found comfort in the fact that someone else had the even more laborious task of cross-referencing the statements. He found out nothing of interest but was hopeful that, when checked, the statements would show up a piece of conflicting evidence that might prove interesting.

He timed his last interview so as not to be left with the last person in line, and when he was finished, he filed his last report and left. He told the constable on the gate that he was leaving for the night and headed home.

On the way, Coles stopped for chips and a video to watch after Martin had gone to bed. The shops were only a few hundred yards from his house, so the food had no time to cool, and was still piping hot when he lifted it from the seat of the car.

The lights were off at the front of the house but when he went in, he could hear Martin's records playing in his room. He shouted up the stairs for Martin to come down and get his chips, and after a few moments he did. Closely followed by Boss, who had yet to be fed.

'Sorry about the note,' Coles apologised.

'That's all right,' Martin replied, then took his food and went back upstairs. He didn't come down again that night.

Coles fed the dog and left some food out for the cat. He sat and read the paper while he ate his chips. When his food was gone, he considered going upstairs to try and patch things up with his son but thought it would be better left until morning. Martin was obviously not in a talking mood.

Coles poured himself a cold beer instead and sat down to watch his video, *The Name of the Rose*. It was an old release, but one Coles had not yet seen. It had been recommended by the shop keeper and Coles liked Sean Connery, so he had decided to give it a try.

The cat jumped up on his knee and settled down to sleep and Boss wandered upstairs to find Martin. The cat was John's, and the dog was Martin's. It had always been that way.

ANALYSIS 5

As with the previous, there is generally just more posturing and positioning within this chapter. There is a scattering of new names taken from school friends and St Philip's choir members listed on their album cover. None of these are really characters of substance within the story and are just name checked as a nod to the past.

The reference to the film *The Name of the Rose* was included as it was a very high-profile film around this time, and I remember some schoolyard banter that the sex scene was actually real. I mean it could have been, but this was a long time pre-digital, and VHS was rubbish paused or in slow-mo. You always got those fuzzy lines across the screen, and they were guaranteed to be exactly where you didn't need them.

Having a quick search on the Internet I can find no reference to this rumour now, so I am not sure where it originated but there is plenty of commentary around the film.

One interesting fact is that Sean Connery's career was at such a low point some funding was withdrawn when he was cast. Even more interestingly, Christian Slater was apparently only fifteen when his sex scene was filmed, which makes it seemingly less likely the rumour that it was real was true. I'm sure even the 1980s Hollywood deviants (that we have recently learnt existed in droves) didn't put their sexual misdemeanours on general release. According to IMDB he didn't use a butt double though. Go Christian!

The next standout for me, at the end of this chapter, is the appearance of a dog when Coles gets home to Martin, a cat too - but that's neither here nor there due to feline independence. The reason it stands out is that I know the dog becomes relevant later in the story, and this must have been the point that I realised I needed a dog and included one. If I had been more proficient, I would have gone back to the early chapter when Martin had been fishing with his dad and introduced the dog then, but there is no mention of it, either with them while they fish or waiting for them when they return home.

Said dog was also based on a real-life hound, at least I intended it to be. I have called the dog Boss in the story, and at the time of writing I believed this to be the dog of the aforementioned Darren Hall, the friend I wish I had known for longer. Trawling both my memory and my scribblings, I cannot say for certain this dog was called Boss, or that he even existed at all.

I also question the name as I have some vague recollection that the dog may have actually been called Boz, a reference to Charles Dickens. It seems unlikely my mind has crafted this as a false memory, much more likely I initially thought someone called the dog Boss and I didn't correct my notes when I realised the error. The wider mystery is that I have no recollection of ever having seen a dog with Darren. Was the whole thing imagined?

And as if by magic, although thoroughly true, I have crafted a perfect segue to another episode of my childhood.

I will start with a little refresher, and we can get back to the dog in due course. My entry into the world took place in Malta on 19th July 1970. I very nearly exited the world shortly thereafter when my mother tripped on her flipflop while carrying me down the stairs of our apartment. When questioned about this incident in adulthood, she had no real explanation why she thought letting go of me to grab the banister and save herself was the better option. Let's give her the benefit of the doubt and just call it survival instinct.

Her screams brought out one of the neighbours, and fortunately he was a young doctor. He checked me over and it seemed there was no harm done, I was a chubby little bouncing baby boy it seems. Interestingly, I am told by my parents this young doctor was Adrian Bianchi who would later go on to be one of the surgeons involved in the controversial separation of Maltese Siamese twins, Gracie & Rosie Attard.

On reading, the Attard twins were separated after the medical team sought court approval against the parents' wishes. Approval was granted on grounds that without intervention both twins were likely to die, something the parents were prepared to leave for God's will due to their religious beliefs. Following a failed appeal, surgery proceeded in the knowledge that Rosie would not survive, as she was wholly dependent on Gracie's heart for her circulation. Rosie died on 7th November 2020, at 12:10am, her sister survived and still has a 'pleasant relationship' with Mr Bianchi, the papers report.

Following my encounter with Mr Bianchi, I survived to be the third child and first son for my parents, with two sisters aged six and four at the time. Although, as a small teaser, I will need to come back and clarify this statement later in the story…

We had left Malta long before my second birthday, so I have no personal recollection of the place, although I do still feel bizarrely attached. I have been back only once, on a working trip, as the island is now quite a hub for near-shoring IT development, and I just felt good about being there. I can't really explain it. I also had a holiday booked last year but the dreaded COVID put paid to that. I will go back again though. I didn't get much tourist time on the work trip so I would love to explore a bit. Hell, the film set for Robin Williams' *Popeye* is still there!

I believe we left the island in haste, due to a bit of political posturing by prime minister Edward Heath. There was some dispute around multi-million-dollar payment demands for use of military compounds, so the decision was made to withdraw the UK military from the area after a 170-year presence. Next stop for our family was RAF Locking, just outside of sunny Weston-Super-Mare.

We moved on again from Locking before I was four, however, I do have some vague recollections from there. We went back at a later date to visit a family friend and I remember a conversation with my mum about something I thought was familiar, and she confirmed I was right, so a few little details must have been lodged back there in my memory somewhere. Locking was also the place where I had my first dog.

Not a real dog, that wouldn't happen until my mid-thirties, my parents were cat people unfortunately. No, this dog was my imaginary friend. Maybe at two years old my imagination couldn't stretch to a fully formed human, so a canine friend was all I could muster, but this imaginary dog was very real to me I am assured.

He existed for the entirety of our stay in Locking, living with us in our flat. I have no name for the little fella, in fact I have no memories of it at all anymore, but I recall conversations about it that took place. My parents are still alive, I could ask them for more detail, but another decision I have made for this exercise is to try and tell the story from my own recollections. I am doing a little bit of research in terms of places and events, such as the Maltese political situation, but I don't want to ask family and friends for their version of events. I really want this story to be my own view.

So, this little doggie was with me always, following me around and being part of my childhood games. So much so that my mother decided to play along and include him herself when playing with me. She spoke to him and pretended to pat his head but became more than a little disturbed when her three-year-old son looked at her with a genuinely puzzled expression, and awkwardly pointed out the dog was on the other side of the room.

Our next RAF posting was to West Drayton, Middlesex. We would stay there for our longest posting of nearly six years, and this is where I would start to have real childhood memories and make my first life-long friend; a real human friend. The dog did not move with us and was not mentioned again, except apparently much later, sometime before my ninth birthday as we would be off to Germany shortly after that.

We were in a gathering of family and friends, and for whatever reason the topic of conversation had come around to dogs. During the course of the conversation, I quite nonchalantly mentioned that I used to have a dog. One of my sisters immediately interjected and refuted my claim. I was insistent, argumentative even, I absolutely swore I had a dog at our previous home. My sister followed this up with my mother, no doubt wanting to prove me wrong, and the whole imaginary dog story resurfaced. Spooky!

I am an absolute sceptic when it comes to anything at all supernatural. I absolutely love horror stories, any ghoulish ghostly hauntings, anything mystical or magical. Timetravel, reincarnation, zombies, psychics. I love it all, and I believe in none of it. Perhaps that is a little inaccurate; I would love to believe in all of it, but I am unprepared to take dubious second-hand accounts as any sort of evidence. The blurred pictures of so-called spectres that still get taken, even though we are living in an age of such high resolution you could photograph a pimple on my arse from outer space.

I think I would be a complete non-believer, but this imaginary dog episode really does capture my imagination. I have a math, physics, computer programming background. I need hard evidence. I need to see the ghost myself. I will believe things when they happen to me, and this one happened to me, so the psychic phenomena door remains ajar.

Confession: despite saying that I would read and review each chapter in turn, I am now reading one chapter ahead of you so I can plan how the analysis sections may sit together. I want to create some natural flow through my life as well as interweave with the fiction of the original story.

The next chapter is very small and potentially uncomfortable reading for any of the PE teachers from my childhood, but I can assure you Mr Davies and his actions are entirely fictional! I will therefore continue my West Drayton years after you have read that, and I have explained it a little further.

The only other thing worthy of mention at this point is that this week I received a phone call from the CFO, my acting line manager while the CTO is currently on maternity leave. She will not be returning; her position is now redundant. Oh, the relief!

You may recall from the preface that I was not a fan. In the short time between her starting with the company until announcing her pregnancy she had created merry hell for me and my team. All with good intentions I am sure, but, in my opinion, with completely the wrong approach and therefore the wrong result. We all knew we weren't where we needed to be, we all knew things could be improved, but there were underlying reasons that she did not take the time to fully understand.

Transformation requires collaboration. You need to take people with you on that journey - lead them into the unknown of which they will be naturally apprehensive. If your role is to march the troops up the side of an icy mountain to greener pastures on the other side, you do it carrot-style from the front, with promises of sunshine and better times to come. You don't stay at the back, stick-style, criticising everyone for being on the wrong side of the mountain in the first place - suggesting if they aren't able to move, they will be left behind. Just my opinion…

To be clear, I wish no misfortune on anyone. I am sure an amicable severance package will have been agreed, and I had a small email interchange in which I passed on my best wishes for the future. Lockdown looks to be coming to an end this summer, our shops will be re-opening from 12th April, with potentially near normality returning from 21st June. Hopefully, this year will be more prosperous for all of us, but I cannot deny, for me personally, the imminent return to the office will undoubtedly be more pleasant following this news.

CHAPTER 6

Jaymi, Michael, and the rest of the boys from their dorm and the other two dorms on the floor filed into the communal bathroom to wash before rest period.

The room was quite large, with sinks the length of the left wall; urinals, toilet cubicles and two bath cubicles along the right wall; an island bench stood in the middle of the floor with clothe hooks; and at the end of the room was an open shower area.

All the boys were clad in only dressing gowns and slippers, with each one carrying a towel and wash bag.

On entering the room, each boy removed his dressing gown and hung it over a peg with his wash bag. Slippers and towel were placed routinely below on the bench. The two boys who were first on the list for a bath went to the bathing cubicles, the rest of the lads had to shower.

A few diverted to use the toilets, the rest made their way to the shower area, each boy reluctant to be the first in, as the water was always freezing to begin with.

Before too long the room was full of steam - somewhat like a sauna house - and the boys were shouting to be heard above the thundering cascade of water.

Some had left the shower and begun to dry themselves. A few, further ahead in their routine, had their dressing gowns and slippers back on and were cleaning their teeth at the sinks.

Michael, who had just finished drying himself, had a mischievous glint in his eye as he twirled his damp towel into a whip shape and dipped the end in a puddle of water on the floor.

As Jaymi left the shower to come over to his towel, Michael pulled back his arm and let crack with his makeshift whip. Jaymi spotted him just at the last minute and turned. The tip of the towel caught him on the top of his leg, and the welt appeared almost before the yelp sounded.

Soon the room descended into chaos as the others joined in. Some grabbed for their dressing gowns to provide a vital layer of protection. Others, engrossed in the battle, carried on naked.

None were more engrossed than Michael and Jaymi. Simon had managed to land a stinging shot on both of their behinds, and they now teamed up and had gone back for revenge.

Neither of the boys had noticed everyone else stop fooling and fall silent. Nor, as they both recoiled their arms and let fly shots that landed simultaneously in Simon's groin, did they notice Mr Davies standing behind them. Simon dropped to the floor, both hands grasping at the pain between his legs.

Mr Davies shouted something as he moved over to where Simon lay. As he passed Michael and Jaymi, now standing rigidly aware of Mr Davies presence, he clipped them both around the head.

'Nobody moves!' he raged, as he knelt before Simon. 'Let's have a look,' he requested, in a more comforting tone.

Simon reluctantly removed his hands to allow inspection. Davies gently slipped his fingers under Simon's scrotum and cupped his hand loosely around his testicles. He squeezed softly then slowly began to probe all around Simon's sack and shaft, asking at intervals if it was tender.

'I think I'm all right sir,' Simon replied, becoming embarrassed by the thorough inspection being performed in full view of his friends.

Davies ignored him and allowed his hand to linger unnecessarily, only withdrawing when it became obvious Simon's swelling was not all as a result of the wound.

'Right! I want you all back in your dorms in five minutes,' Davies said as he stood up, allowing Simon to scurry away and cover himself. 'Michael! Jaymi! Come with me,' he added.

They both moved to grab their gowns, but Davies stopped them.

'As you are,' he said.

Both boys looked at each other's nakedness, then back to Mr Davies.

'I'll make you do a circuit of the school like that if you don't hurry up.'

They both scurried after him, aware that his threats were seldom idle.

He marched them up the corridor to their dorm, and there he made them stand, one each side of the door, with their backs against the wall and their hands by their sides.

When all the other boys had returned to their dorms, Davies fetched himself a chair from the end of the corridor. He placed it not far from the boys and sat himself down, and there they stayed for almost the full hour of the rest period. Mr Davies only allowed them to return to the bathroom for their belongings five minutes before lights-out.

Nothing more was said.

ANALYSIS 6

My life experiences, certainly until adulthood, have always been easy to compartmentalise. Even in adulthood I still use the technique to recall events. What house I was living in, what relationship I was in, what car did I have at the time. Any thread really that helps to pinpoint the moment in time. I guess everyone does this to some degree but during my childhood and adolescence as an air force child, it was extremely easy to do this, as each compartment of time tends to end very abruptly with little continuity.

Although you know another move is only a few years away, you don't dwell on it and when the date is announced by your father it seems to be with relatively short notice. Not a major issue most of the time (we'll come back to my teenage rage later) as, if you weren't moving away, then all your friends would be at some point, so you'd still be starting again, one way or another.

Each compartment of time starts with you arriving as the new boy in your street, the new boy in your school, and ends again, with all the friends you've made and the routines you've developed being lost. Just memories now, from a specific period which I've tagged in my mind with the name of the relevant country or RAF base.

Malta, RAF Locking, RAF West Drayton, Germany, RAF Abingdon, and RAF Brize Norton. These six postings for my father defined my whole life up to and including the time when the Murder at St Philip's story was created. My father left the RAF after Brize Norton, and my days as a military gypsy came to an end. I still love to travel for holidays, but thirty years after my father's work stopped us moving around, I still live only four miles away from the base at which he finished his career.

The St Philip's shower scene, as with most elements of the story, was crafted from a combination of experiences. I have already explained the residential trip to Wales which was a clear influence from my 'Abingdon' years, and I believe other elements were influenced from a film I watched in my very early twenties, *The Boys of St Vincent*.

This was a harrowing true-life story of child abuse at a Catholic run orphanage in Canada. I am normally dubious of true stories; far too cynical that the movie makers will have used too much poetic licence for the purpose of entertainment. In this case I don't think it matters. If not every fact is pinpoint accurate in this specific tale, I think that the Catholic church has been proven to be eminently culpable of equally horrific atrocities on many other occasions.

Strangely, it wasn't actually the abusive storyline that merited its inclusion in my story, either then or now. I was more influenced by the nudity. I mentioned before that when I am writing I am always visualising everything (perhaps I should be attempting a screenplay rather than a novel!) and as I visualised my story it seemed sensible there would be nudity in the showers at a boy's school.

At the time I would have been confidently imagining my story would at least get made into a television drama, and when it did, and I was working alongside the director, I would be insisting the nudity was non-negotiable. I can't imagine any UK production company would have allowed nudity of minors, even back then, but I really believed in realism.

The St Vincent movie was French/Canadian so that probably had some influence on that production, and many of my other favourite films are European. *Au Revoir les Enfants*; Louis Malle's biographical boarding school tale where the teachers are hiding a Jewish boy from the Nazi's, or *Le Grand Chemin*; another tale of life where if a rabbit need skinning, they just skin one on camera, no need for special effects. This is life, this is what happens. And as I grew older, *La Vita è Bella*, *Cinema Paradiso*, *La Mala Educación*... the list goes on and on of excellent filmmaking without the need for airbrushing.

Fleeting nudity is not porn, and I almost think the avoidance of it at all costs adds to the danger of it being considered sexualised. This doesn't happen in Europe and maybe my exposure to European television when living in Germany is what shaped my thinking.

Don't get me wrong, I am advocating innocence and normality and nothing more. I am fully aware protection needs to be paramount, I grew up in the seventies and eighties. Jimmy Saville, Rolf Harris, Stuart Hall, these were my childhood TV stars. Gary Glitter, Michael Jackson, they were music icons. Well, perhaps Gary Glitter wasn't an icon, and I realise Michael Jackson remains innocent, but you get the idea. More recently there has been the #Metoo movement exposing the Hollywood casting-couch culture. Even the Royal family are reported to be complicit. All of this is obviously atrocious and needs to be stopped, but I still don't think a flash of a naked bottom exiting a shower is going to corrupt us all.

The Boys of St Vincent did not actually get released until I was twenty-one but at that stage, I was still revising the St Philip's story I had begun when I was seventeen. I had reengineered it on occasion, added whole sections in areas to try and pad out the word count. I had converted it from handwritten notes to a typed manuscript, then onto my Amstrad word processor, and then later on to my first windows PC. At the start of this new incarnation, I have first had to import all the old Microsoft Word files onto my MacBook. How time and technology flies!

Despite the clear influences, I feel I should clarify just one more time, Mr Davies and his doings in this chapter are totally fictional. I believe this chapter was a later addition to the story and was positioned to bring Mr Davies character into question. This is a murder story after all, and in good old Jessica Fletcher style, we need some suspects before we arrive at the final conclusion.

Awkward nudity talk over, I will now return to the chronology of my life. Before I do, I must just mention the very heavy use of the semi-colon in the second paragraph. Not sure where that came from, maybe I had been reading up on grammar, although I still have no idea now if it is the correct usage.

We have arrived at compartment three of my childhood, RAF West Drayton. Before here, I think any memories I have are just memories of things I have been told. From West Drayton onwards I definitely have my own memories. We lived here a little longer than the usual posting of three years. Almost six years, due to a double posting I assume, if such a thing exists.

I actually believe my earliest memory is first pulling up at the kerbside in front of our new house following the move from Locking, but I know my mother doubted this when I mentioned it. She questioned if maybe I just remembered coming home from one of our annual Cornish holidays. I can't be sure, but neither can anyone else so let's assume my memories start there.

My second memory can't be from much later as it involves my nursery school. I don't recall the name, but I know it was in a church building overlooking a playing green on a housing estate just a short walk up from the Yiewsley Parade shops.

This green would be a regular feature, of my weekdays at least, for years to come as I would need to walk past it to get to Cherry Lane Primary school where I would move up to after nursery. We were allowed to walk to school alone back then, we weren't yet conscious to the fact Jimmy or Rolf may be on the prowl.

I also recall this little grassy area being piled high with rubbish bags during the strikes of the seventies - presumably this was the 1978/79 winter of discontent - so much later than my nursery days. The memory of the nursery may also have been after I had actually stopped attending, it's vague in my mind but I recall it as it was quite sad. A couple living in the building both died.

I do not recall much more than that, I assume it would not have been discussed very much with me at that young age, but as with many memories there are little inklings of things I'm sure I know. If pushed, I would suggest they died from carbon monoxide poisoning from a faulty boiler, and if pushed further I might say they had a son my age who I knew. Whatever the truth, something stayed with me.

There are many more happier memories from those years - the Christmas tree fire aside - so I will rattle through a few, and dwell on some others before we move on from this section of my history.

School was obviously a big part of my life in those days, and this would be one of only two times in my six-school life when I would not be the only person starting as the new boy, the second being the move up to my first secondary school in Germany. I don't have any particular recollection of my first day, but I recall all sorts of little details. Early years classes in Portacabins, moving up to the bigger classes in the main school. The playground was also separated by a diagonal white line to keep the children similarly segregated during breaks.

I remember warm milk on radiators and noisy playtimes, snippets of lessons and the smell of the purple-inked photostat worksheets. The pull-out wooden gym frames and climbing ropes used for PE lessons in the hall, which also multi-tasked for assemblies and lunchtimes. I remember the roar of low-flying aircraft due to the school's location on the Heathrow flightpath, and there were blackboard-eraser throwing teachers, Mr Scarfogliero having a particularly good aim if you failed to give him your full attention in class.

The ultimate sanction was a visit to the headmaster's office, which everyone knew still sported a cane.

I fell afoul on one occasion, which merited a trip to the headmaster's office following a mischievous playtime prank with a friend called Alan. For whatever reason we were the first two through the doors to the main building when the rain started to fall, and I thought it would be a good idea to bolt the door behind us, leaving all the other lower school students and teachers stuck in the rain. Oh, how we laughed - until we were summoned to the headmaster's office. Actually, something is telling me it may have been a headmistress, either way, we were petrified.

We were made to sit outside the office for what seemed like an age, convinced we were about to be whipped. We were only around seven years old, but we managed to hold ourselves together enough not to cry while we waited. When we were finally ushered in it was all a very welcome anticlimax. There was no cane, not even a telling off. We were asked why we were there and then dismissed back to our classroom after being told, despite her having the memory of an elephant, that she did not recall the incident. With hindsight, a combination of urban myth and the time waiting nervously outside the office, was all the punishment required.

Recalling this story has brought something else to mind I had never really thought about before. I have never tended to mix my school friends with my out of school friends, for which I now have a theory I will return to later. If I had, then Michael Oram would almost certainly have been my partner in crime at school as he was my best friend throughout the West Drayton years. As it was, we were not in the same class at school, so our adventures took place in an around our homes on Rutters Close.

I do remember we would walk back home from school together, meeting one or other of our mothers on the way. My own mother worked in the NAAFI club on the RAF camp and that was about halfway on the mile or so walk home. We would usually stop at the local shop for a bag of 10p mix, and let me tell you some of those sweets were four-a-penny back then so it was a good size bag of sweets, which invariably I would have finished before we got back home.

Rutters Close was a small estate off-camp used for military housing. If you took an aerial view as you entered the close, you would find it roughly in the shape of an uppercase 'E', with the entrance being in the bottom left corner of the letter. Both Michael and I lived at the far end of the first prong of the E, and at the top right-hand end you would find a NAAFI shop, which actually backed on to the RAF camp - although there was no access to the base itself.

At the tip of both the first and second prongs there was a field and play park, both of which sat alongside the railway lines. I would later discover this was the mainline into Paddington from Oxford, and as a commuter I would often see my old house flash past. The nostalgia had faded though as the play parks had been covered in additional housing and it all looked rather sad. I knew this already; I had returned there once. I'll come back to it, but my advice is to just keep the memories alive in your mind, nowhere is ever the same when you return after so many years.

In the nineteen seventies, however, this was our playground. As you would expect, my rose-tinted memory only recalls glorious sunny days in which we played outside for hours on end. To be fair, 1976 did bring us one of the hottest summers on record back then, but I am sure it rained too at some point of my childhood. In fact, I know it did, mostly in Cornwall when we were on holiday.

Our imaginations crafted much better games then, than any software creator has managed on a console since. There are far too many to list here, but I will capture just a few, including our most outstanding achievement before we move on. If we weren't in the park, we would be racing down footpaths on our bikes, the mandatory playing card held in the spokes by a peg to give full motorbike sound effects of course. Or we would be in our gardens re-enacting our favourite TV programs. *Hawaii Five-0*, *The Streets of San Francisco*, *The Hardy Boys*, *The Six Million Dollar Man*, *Dr Who*; they all got our treatment. I am told that on the American shows we would even insert breaks for end of part one… before going back to our game after the imaginary adverts had finished.

Star Wars cannot be forgotten, it was a big deal for any '70s child. We collected the figurines, or more to the point, we played with them. I am sure that if we had collected them, and left them pristine in their boxes, they would be worth something now. My current job (although if this book gets published it may well be my previous job unless I heavily edit the preface) is in the toy industry and there is still a fascination with *Star Wars* and the collectables all these years later due to the various prequels, sequels, and spinoffs. Out of interest, I have just googled the *Star Wars* franchise earnings, and it has apparently made over $10 billion at the box office alone.

I remember on one of the walks home from school, early 1978, my father pulled up alongside in his strata blue Vauxhall Viva. This was extremely unusual as he should have been at work, but he had finished early to take me to the cinema, probably in Uxbridge or Slough, to see the new *Star Wars: Episode IV* film. A memory that has stayed with me, bar the small period of doubt I mentioned earlier when I convinced myself my father had been absent from my childhood. Sorry Dad.

This is also a memory I replicated in 1999, when I took my own son to see the newly released *Star Wars: Episode I*. Aaron was just little younger than I had been, and Jar Jar Binks was no Luke Skywalker, but all the same it was a parallel event in time that touched my heart, in 1978, in 1999, and still now.

Enough of the sloppiness, let's get back to the real triumph of my seventies. Six months before *Star Wars* was released, the Silver Jubilee was celebrated with a full-on day of events and a street party, as you might expect amongst the RAF community. During this day of fun and competition there was a parade, fancy dress, and Morris dancing, among all manner of things but we had our eye on a particular prize.

There was to be a wheelbarrow race for our age group, from which Michael and I would emerge victorious. I remember the whole thing in glorious slow-motion. Michael had held my ankles and pushed me down the outbound stretch before switching places for the return leg. I pushed with all my might, looking down on Michael, now in the wheelbarrow position in a white and green rugby shirt that I can still picture vividly. We had not been leading on the turn but as arms weakened and bodies collapsed, we kept strong and powered through to glory. I still have my commemorative Silver Jubilee coin somewhere in a cupboard.

As strong as the memories are, and as fun as it all was, just over a year later Michael would have moved away, and another six months or so later still, I would have moved on to Germany. Another compartment of my childhood closed off and another one about to begin. Previous routines become memories and best friends are lost. Brutal! Although Michael would not be lost forever…

CHAPTER 7

Outside the wind blew hard and cold against the newly fitted windows of Coles's home. Well, the estate agent had had the foresight to see it as a home, but to Coles it was merely four walls in need of a great deal more than a lick of paint to give it the warmth of any previous home he had occupied. As for the double-glazing, Coles had been on at the fitters for weeks to come back and finish the plastering. It was new however, which was one up on the rest of the building.

It was at times like these that Coles wondered if the house would just blow down around him. From the day he had moved in, pieces of thatch had been falling from the roof for seemingly no reason, but when the storms came, not a straw could be found on the ground. Whether this was because none fell, or that the ones which did were blown away on the breeze Coles did not know, nor did he care. At this moment, the roof was the furthest from Coles' mind in more sense than one.

A bottle had just smashed outside the back door. Not unusual; the cat was always breaking the empty milk bottles and would have been blamed for this one too had she not been curled up on John's lap, sound asleep. As soundly as a cat ever sleeps.

Must have been the dog.

As soon as the thought had crossed his mind, Boss had come walking down the stairs from his usual sleeping place at the foot of Martin's bed. So much for that theory.

The wind! Now that was definitely outside.

It seemed like a reasonable explanation and more importantly it put Coles' mind at rest. He had spent the whole day on the trail of a murderer and did not much fancy the idea of spending the night trying to track down the phantom bottle smasher. The wind it was.

Coles relaxed once more in the reclining chair he had bought for his wife when she was pregnant with Martin, a bit tatty now but still comfortable, and in minutes was asleep again.

John's eyes opened suddenly, and he sat up with a jerk. The cat had just sunk her claws into his leg and was proceeding to pull herself along the length of his lap.

'Bitch!' Coles shouted as he threw the cat to the floor.

The cat was as startled as Coles had been and ran for cover under the sofa, wondering what she had done wrong.

The television was still on, but the transmission had finished hours ago. The remote control was out of reach, so Coles forced himself up out of the chair and across the room to the set. The switch gave a loud click as it was released.

Coles walked away from the set only to hear the click repeated. Not once, but continuously. He turned back to face the television and found he was mistaken; the sound no longer came from the set, nor was it a click. The sound he could now hear was more of a tapping and seemed to be coming from the kitchen.

The door to the kitchen was shut tight but Coles managed to open it without a sound. He suddenly had visions of all the films he had seen in which people walked around in the dark searching for intruders. In an instant he realised their insanity and slipped his hand through the door and along the wall to the light switch.

As he stepped into the room, he noticed the back door was open. He moved cautiously towards it, his heart beating heavily. He stopped as he reached the door and looked out. He gave a brief sigh of relief when he saw the cause of the tapping.

The washing line Coles had hung from the side of the house across to the shed had snapped, and the flailing end was tapping against the window of the shed.

Coles tied back the line and the noise was gone. His heartbeat slowed and he walked back into the kitchen through the door he had now forgotten was open when he first entered the room.

He looked around to reassure himself everything was alright and was about to leave when he noticed the microwave. The counter showed five seconds and was counting down. Coles moved closer and as he stood in front of the machine the counter reached zero. The bell rang and the light came on.

John's heart missed a beat. When he caught his breath, he began to scream. Sitting in a dish in the microwave was Martin's severed head. Blood filled the bowl and Martin's eyes stared blindly out at Coles.

Michael had been unable to sleep in much more than twenty-minute bursts and, at the moment, lay awake staring at the ceiling of the dorm. The rest of the school was silent and as Michael lay awake, he tried to imagine how the classes would look dark and empty.

The silence was occasionally broken as one of Michael's dorm mates rolled over in their sleep, but soon returned as they found a more comfortable sleeping position and settled down again.

Michael had almost dozed off when he was brought back to consciousness by Jaymi coughing. Jaymi also woke himself and saw Michael was awake with his head lifted from the pillow and looking in Jaymi's direction.

'Are you awake Jaymi?' Michael asked quietly so as not to wake the others.

'Yeah!' Jaymi replied from the darkness. 'Did I wake you up?'

'No. I've been awake all night. I was thinking about McWinney.'

'What about him?' Jaymi asked, now sitting up in his bed.

Michael saw Jaymi sit up so climbed out of his own bed and went over and sat on the end of his friends.

'What if the killer is still in the school?' Michael whispered. 'He might kill someone else.'

Jaymi could only see Michael's outline, silhouetted by the moonlight that shone through the window behind him, but could sense the fear on his friend's face. Michael was scared and had come to Jaymi for reassurance. Jaymi found it

106

hard to believe that Michael needed his advice, but at the same time was flattered that the boy everyone saw as leader of the year, was only twelve like the rest of them, and had turned to Jaymi to talk too.

'So, what if he is?' Jaymi said. 'People kill for a reason, and there's no reason why they'd want to kill us is there?'

'What if someone saw them push McWinney through the window?'

'Well, as long as the killer never saw them then they're safe, but if he did see them, well then they might worry, but we were outside when it happened so it's not our problem to worry about is it?'

'I suppose you're right. They'd be pretty stupid to try and kill them when they were in their dorm anyway. The other boys might wake up.'

'Right!' Jaymi agreed. 'What have we got first lesson tomorrow?' he added, trying to change the subject.

'English, then PE' Michael answered.

'You'll get to skip football again you lucky shit.'

'I guess I owe Richard one for that,' Michael said, then wished he had not. Jaymi was always on at him about his pen pal, so Michael tried to avoid mentioning him.

'About Richard, I'm sorry about what I said earlier, and all the other times,' Jaymi hesitated then continued his apology with his head bowed. 'I haven't got any friends away from school, and the way you go on about him I thought you were best mates, and I always thought we were best mates. I guess I'm just jealous.'

Michael could not believe his ears. He remained silent for a moment, then spoke.

'You are my best mate. I only see Richard in the holidays, he's just a friend. Jealous?' Michael repeated in disbelief.

'Anyway, you had better go back to your bed,' Jaymi said sounding a little embarrassed. 'If the others see you here talking about being jealous of other men they'll start to talk.'

Both boys laughed quietly, and Michael stood up and walked back to his bed. As he reached the end, he turned back to face Jaymi and thanked him for the chat. Michael fell straight to sleep after that, and both he and Jaymi dreamt of each other that night. Something had happened in their ten-minute talk that had made their friendship much stronger. They would be friends for the rest of their lives.

Coles had turned his head away from the microwave, but the image of his son's face was still etched clearly in his mind. The bell still sounded in the background, but the tone had changed.

Suddenly Coles opened his eyes and looked around to see the familiar four walls of his bedroom. The bell he could hear was his alarm clock on the bedside table. He switched it off and relaxed back into the pillows.

The dream had been so realistic. It was not the first time he had dreamt of losing Martin, but it was certainly the worst. John decided the present tension between them was more than likely the cause, and he vowed to patch things up over breakfast.

He washed and dressed then went downstairs, stopping on the way to check Martin was in his bed, head attached. He was, much to John's relief.

Martin came down the stairs shortly after his father and joined him in the kitchen for a silent breakfast. As far as he was concerned, they were still not talking.

Coles had to speak first.

'I'm sorry about yesterday. I didn't want to leave you again, but I had to. It's my job.'

'And I'm your son,' Martin snapped back.

'I know, and I love you Martin, but we need to find a compromise.'

'I love you too Dad, but it hurts when you leave me after promising to take me out.'

Coles was touched. Martin had never told him he loved him since he was about five, and that was probably just because he wanted something.

'Right! How about we finish breakfast, and after that I've got to go to work.'

Martin's face dropped.

'But,' John continued, 'how about I take you with me?'

Martin looked up in disbelief. If there was one thing he wanted to do, it was to go to work with his dad, but he had never expected to be allowed to.

'Okay, eat your toast and get dressed, we've got a busy day ahead. First, we have to go to the station, then we're going to school. St Philip's that is, not yours.'

Coles was glad his son was happy, but what would the Super say when he found out he had taken his son out on a murder investigation?

ANALYSIS 7

I seem to have become a little out of sync between fiction and fact at the moment, as autobiographically I am just about to begin my time in Germany, however, the start of this fictional chapter seven is bedded firmly in the next period of my life, back in England after the German years come to an end.

That said, there has already been a degree of bouncing around in time and I think this is only likely to continue as we pass the point in time when the fiction was written and on through my twenties, thirties, and forties until we arrive back where this whole project started. Fifty and in full midlife crisis.

Coles' nightmare sequence is routed firmly in the love of horror books and films I developed in my teens, and no self-respecting horror story would be complete without a dream sequence. My particular favourite being in *An American Werewolf in London*, which I watched at a much younger age than I should have. They catch you out twice with a double-layered dream sequence that wouldn't be out of place in Inception.

It was mostly books though where my love of this genre began. Robin Cook, James Herbert, Stephen King were all favourites of my teenage years, a progression from The Famous Five stories I had previously loved, and before those my Rupert Bear annuals. My literary taste changed again a few years later but I will touch on that in due course. Needless to say, I have always loved reading.

When I started writing my own book, I had every intention it would be a full-blown novel and I suspect certain sections, such as my horror diversion, were there purely to pad out the pages. I am still satisfied how I managed to use even the padding to engineer other elements of the story, such as Coles' agreeing to take Martin to work. I did not do a very good job though as, even with the padding, I had only managed to craft a novella at best.

If I were to revisit and rewrite the story, and maybe I will as a future project, I feel there is so much more I could now bring to the story that could stretch it to the novel I had intended. Not least of all I could do some research and make some of the practical elements more realistic. I assume taking your son to work when you are a police officer is not really acceptable behaviour, but I wasn't researching it for a gritty real-life detective story at the time. I needed Martin at the school to facilitate another element of my story, so I wrote him there, it really was that simple.

The interaction between Michael and Jaymi is much more aligned to my time in Germany and reflects the kind of conversation I would have had with my best friend of that period, certainly in the later part of those years. Not in content but in the sense conversations were maturing, capable of sensitivity, and friendships were becoming more serious, more meaningful, harder to lose.

Not a lot more in chapter seven worth dwelling on before we get into the fun and the heartbreak of Germany, but I did notice a treble of oddities. There is a reference to Michael's broken arm being something to do with Richard. I know why I included the feature, my friend Darren had a broken arm when I was getting to know him, but I have reread the first few chapters, where the broken arm is also referred to, and there is no mention of how Michael came to have one. I am trying to remember if this is revealed later in the story, but I truly don't remember. I hope it is, otherwise, I missed a great padding opportunity.

The second spot is a potential continuity error, but I could maybe overlook it, and certainly could explain it away in any rewrite. When Michael is having his little 'me time' in the abandoned top floor of the building this scene must have somehow taken place between the bell ringing for end of lessons and him meeting Jaymi outside where they witnessed the fall. Jaymi did have to stay behind to retry the robes Mrs Beavis had been altering, and I appreciate teenage boys can be over and done relatively swiftly, but he still had to get there and get back, via the toilets, so the timing does feel a little tight.

The third thing I noticed is just a straightforward error. In chapter seven Michael is said to be twelve years old but I have already aged him as thirteen earlier in the story. It is suggested the boys are in their second year at the school and Michael is described as one of the oldest in his year, so I think thirteen sounds more likely. I am almost certainly going to need a good editor if my writings are ever to see the light of day.

Back to the biography. I'm now nine years old and life has taken me to Germany. I previously talked of how I have compartmentalised my childhood and adolescence in to six segments. Germany is number four of these although it really has a subsection as we also moved within Germany. On arrival we were housed off-base in a flat in Bauxhof, a suburb of Erkelenz allocated for RAF housing but with a very German feel. Later we would move to a married quarter on the main camp, but I'll take each section in turn.

My father drove us over to Germany and although I have some memory of packing up the car to leave, I have very scattered recollections of what must have been quite a long journey. Before we were able to set off on the trip, I do recall my father returning from the RAF march-out inspection which noted my parents had lost an egg spoon during their six-year stay in West Drayton. It seems the military are very precise about this kind of thing and my father probably had the price of this spoon deducted from his salary. I suppose if every member of the forces lost a spoon it would soon add up. I'll remind you of this spoon incident later when another bit of RAF madness would suggest they are not always so careful with their monies.

About the journey itself I think I remember a car ferry, but I couldn't be sure I am not mixing this up with a journey we made back to Northern Ireland to visit family. I do have a specific recollection of a funny conversation though. I remember asking my parents if Germans laughed differently.

A little confused they asked me what I meant, and I explained that if they spoke a different language then when they laughed did that sound different as well. Seemed a sensible question at the time but my parents and sisters seemed to find it hilarious. I remember very little else, I guess I must have slept a lot of the way.

The flat we moved into was great. The whole Bauxhof complex was made up of blocks of six flats, two on each of three floors. We were flat 3, block 33. My lucky number ever since. How lucky I couldn't say, and I am not superstitious at all but when a raffle comes along or one of those pick-a-square-on-a-grid games I am always looking for the number 3, 33, 333, any of those will do.

As you entered the flat, you came in to the first hall. Off this were the kitchen, toilet, and my eldest sisters' bedroom and a fourth door that led into a large lounge/diner. This lounge had a balcony the whole width of it and another door on the opposite side that led into the second hall. From here was the main bathroom and three other bedrooms for my parents, my middle sister and me. The block also had a cellar, and each flat had a storage lock-up down there.

There were other novelties too. The windows opened inwards for ease of cleaning, and wheelie bins. These may not seem like much, but this was 1979, it would be another twenty-five years before we got a wheelie bin in England, and I suspect we still don't fit inward opening upstairs windows as standard to this day. It was a great flat, an apartment really, calling it a flat just doesn't seem to do it justice.

My best friend during the German years was Eugene McCluskey and he lived upstairs in the same block. He had arrived just before us and we would both move up to the main camp at roughly the same time too, so this friendship was continuous though my time in Germany. He was my out of school friend of course, we didn't share the same class at Merlin Primary or later when we moved up to Kent Secondary.

We had the greatest of adventures during the Bauxhof days. Weekdays it was all about heading up to the bus stop to catch the military green school bus onto the camp where Merlin school was located. School days were longer then too, so by the time we got back home we probably had a little kick about before tea and that would be the end of the day. It was all about the weekends.

I am not sure if our parents knew, or if we just didn't ask, but we seemed to have amazing freedom when we were living there. We were only nine, Eugene may have turned ten before we left, but we would wander off for hours and miles on end. Earlier I touched on our escapade on the frozen lake, so much fun but with hindsight crazily dangerous, but that was just one of many adventures.

We discovered play parks amongst local houses, we wandered off with our pocket money to the large hypermarkets we had never seen the likes of in England and discovered Haribo Goldbears for the first time. There was a local German woman who sold a small selection of ice-creams from her back door, and every bus-stop or local shop seemed to have a selection of candy machines outside. The ones where you pop your coin, ten or twenty pfennigs in this case, in the top of the handle and twist it until your treat is dispensed below.

As well as exploring outside there was also so much other newness in that six-month period. There was a Corona lemonade man who used to drop off fizzy pop, we got our first remote control TV, and an Atari games console turned up on one of our birthdays or Christmases. I am sure all of this was available in England and if we had stayed in the UK things would have equally progressed but due to the timing of the move, I just associated all this excitement with Germany. I just remember it being the greatest of times, and these times only continued when we moved on to the main camp.

I don't remember a period without Eugene to play with but it is unlikely we moved away from Bauxhof on the same day so I guess there must have been some time without him. There are other names from Bauxhof, Callum and Geraint come to mind, but Eugene was definitely my bestie.

On the main base the married quarters were spread out over quite a large area, but it turned out we didn't live too far apart. Our house was one of the first you came to on Harrier Way, just opposite our primary school. Eugene lived just up the road on possibly Pembroke Close, I'm a bit foggy on that. I know it had an extra bedroom adjoined from the house next door as he was from a large Irish family. There were five kids I believe, maybe even six, I seem to remember twins in there somewhere, but I can't be sure, to be sure.

Although in theory the base offered a safer environment than our flat on the edge of Erkelenz, in reality the perimeter was not secure. We knew of a hole in the chain link fence in a secluded wooded area and we would often slip through it and seek adventure in the local town. I touched on this briefly near the beginning of the story, the walks down abandoned train tracks, feeding deer corn cobs through the fence where they were farmed. I also have memories of climbing large wooden ladders that led up to observation towers in the wooded areas, maybe they were for birdwatching or maybe shooting, I'm not sure but they were high, and we shouldn't have been up them so that made it even more fun in our minds.

When we weren't being mischievous off camp, we would be mischievous on camp. I remember on one occasion we stole a little plastic toy from the NAAFI shop where my mum worked. Unfortunately, one of her friends spotted me and when I was confronted back at home I crumbled under questioning and gave myself up. I never grassed on Eugene though, well, until just now.

We weren't bad kids and would mostly spend our time playing on the various greens and parks on camp or riding our bikes around the streets. In the warmer months we would be swimming at the open-air pool, or going to the cinema, a proper old fashioned Regal style affair, although maybe it wasn't actually old fashioned then.

I remember kicking my heels and waiting around on Sunday mornings for Eugene to get back from Sunday school so the adventures could start, which in turn reminds me we used to mess about singing some of the hymns he had learned, mischievously changing the words. Maybe this is where my love of choir music originated. These routines went on throughout our remaining year at primary school and into our time at Kent Secondary until the fateful day came for us to part.

Eugene's dad was posted first, and I remember that sinking feeling all too well. The process at that time was to move out of your allocated house into an accommodation block for the last week or so while you were waiting for transport to your next destination. I would still see Eugene as normal, as this block was just opposite the house they had been in, but before too long the last day came.

I remember being there as they all loaded into the car, one of those big estates with rear facing seats in the boot. We said our goodbyes and then they drove away leaving me waving from the curb-side as the tears started to fall. Over the years I have done the odd social media search for Eugene, but I have always drawn a blank, when he left that day, it was forever. I was heartbroken.

With a stiff upper lip life goes on, and so it did for me. I had other friends but none as close as Eugene, and we didn't stay in Germany that much longer ourselves to build any further deep connections. I did have some close friends at Kent school, Andrew, and Andy to name two, but I won't go into those school days in particular as they are featuring heavily enough throughout as they are the key source for the St Philip's story, Andrew actually not being too far away from the fictional Andrew character in fact.

I will, however, take the opportunity to go over my theory on my friend groups as there is an exception to my own logic here. I said before I seem to have different friends at school to those I have outside of school. I don't know if this is unusual or not, but the fact popped into my head as I trawled the memory banks, so I have been giving it some more thought than usual.

Potentially in my early life it was just a matter of proximity, the school had a wide catchment area, and I would only be able to play with the kids around my own housing estate. It feels like there was more than this though and as I got older, I have a theory that it was more to do with a conflict between intellect and attraction.

I was never the smartest at school, but I was a pretty good allrounder - languages aside. I was in a few top sets and was one of the handful that took their maths O-level early, getting an 'A' I might add. As a result, the classmates I spent most of my time with were all similar, and we got on, like minds and all that. The thing is, we didn't really have like minds.

In the black and white spectrum of education, science versus art, I was definitely on the science side. Good at math, science, technology and poor at art, languages, drama. All very stereotypical but, despite my leanings, I really wanted to be on the other side of the fence. I felt artistic, poetic, creative and I think, in general, I chose those type of people to hang around with outside of school. In addition, there tends to be a generalisation that the science type students are cleverer, and maybe that also plays into my nature. I mentioned earlier I have a mildly controlling nature and perhaps that's easier to enact if your friend group perceive you as more intelligent.

Taking this a little further, I think my father has exactly the same personality trait. Perhaps his decision to stop climbing when he hit the ceiling of non-officer ranks in the RAF was explainable with the big fish little pond analogy. Maybe I am overanalysing.

My little breach of the unwritten rule involved my school friend Andy. We blurred the line, taking our friendship outside of the classroom, and I mention it because of a humorous incident that occurred one weekend which has always stuck in my mind.

Andy's father was not in the RAF, he was living in Germany working as a civilian and lived off camp in a lovely German village, the name of which I cannot recall. Andy went to Kent, as it was an English-speaking school, and we had been friends from the start of our first year. Our friendship strengthened nearer the end of my time in Germany, perhaps after Eugene left, and one weekend I went to stay with him at his home. I took my weekend bag to school on the Friday morning and went home on his school bus instead of mine. We then had the whole weekend together before returning to school on Monday morning.

Their home was stunning compared to our own RAF house, stunning full stop really. A stone-built bungalow with rooms spurring off a large central family area, with an enormous high-ceilinged cellar which housed the utility area and some additional play space. It was set in a beautiful German farming village and during my stay we went on walks, spent some time with Andy's German friends playing pool in the back room of a local bar, and took a visit to the local pig farm.

It was on the Sunday evening, however, the most memorable event of the weekend occurred. It was to be an early night, ready for school again the next day, and I had taken up the offer of having a bath before getting ready for bed. I was merrily splashing away minding my own business when the bathroom door opened, and Andy's mum walked in to announce she had come to wash my hair.

I sat bolt upright, cupped my hands to my crotch and sat there in silence while my hair was washed, conditioned, and rinsed clean. I was only twelve, but I had been washing my own hair for some time now and my parents did not join me when I bathed. I didn't mention it to Andy or anyone else for that matter, perhaps everyone else did this and my family were the exception. Despite my shock it was not an unpleasant experience at all, and I still love to have my hair washed to this day, although it is usually when I am having my hair cut and, as a rule, I tend to be fully clothed.

As my German years were drawing to a close, literally in the last few weeks before we moved, puberty was starting to take a hold. Not yet the firm grip of sprouting hair and breaking voices, but the light touch of self-awareness and an interest in others too. There had been a period of 'you show me yours and I'll show you mine' with a boy my age who lived a few doors away, and in the final week before we moved back home, while living in the same transit block that Eugene had stayed in before his departure, I took an interest in doing the same with a girl I knew.

It only happened a couple of times, once in the woods where she hitched up her skirt and I bent over for a genuinely interested inspection, before I then pulled my trousers and pants to my knees and pushed my groin forwards so she could get a look at my little pecker which, although still pale and small, had stiffened and poked upwards, as was its wont.

The second occasion took place in my room at the hostel and was pretty much a repeat event with an added element of touching. I was clearly thinking about these things a lot as shortly afterwards I awoke in the night lying face down and thrusting my groin against the sheets of the bed. I had the strangest but most pleasant of feelings and rushed off to the bathroom across the corridor as I was concerned I needed to pee really bad. As you can imagine, I did not need to pee at all and, as I held myself and realised I could maintain the good feeling by thrusting through my fingers, I very quickly experienced my first ejaculation.

I couldn't be certain, but if I had stayed in Germany much longer, I feel our exploring would have gone further and further, ending who knows where. I could easily imagine having been one of those unlucky young teenage fathers, caught out by the lethal combination of eagerness and naivety. Ironically, if that had happened, a teenage father would not have been too out of place at my next school.

The return to England took us to RAF Abingdon, Oxfordshire and my school would be Fitzharrys Comprehensive. Christ, I was going to be coming down to earth with a bump, moving back from a military school to this place. My childhood innocence had literally come to an end in Germany, and the next chapter would be my adolescence for sure.

CHAPTER 8

More snow had fallen overnight and the boys in Mr Davies class felt sure they had a good case for indoor sport. Davies, however, was a great believer in outdoor sport no matter what the weather, and being the teacher, he naturally had his way.

'There's too much snow on the ground to play football today,' one of the lads pointed out.

'That's why we're playing rugby,' Davies replied with a smile.

'RUGBY!' Came back the horrified chorus.

The boys begrudgingly donned their shorts and shirts and started to trot out of the changing room.

Michael sat with a smile on his face watching his friends change, then followed them as they, one by one, stepped out into the cold winter air.

On the last half-term holiday Michael had been messing around with Richard at home and had fallen awkwardly and broken his arm. It was still in plaster, so he had been excused from games for the rest of the term.

Michael exited the building last, carrying a string bag full of rugby balls.

'Christ! It's cold out here, I'll just go and get my blazer,' he said to Jaymi, still grinning.

Jaymi returned a dirty look before running off towards the pitch, trying to warm himself up.

Davies had all the boys doing warm up exercises before they started the match. Carl insisted on playing the fool as usual, but soon stopped when threatened with sit ups in the snow. After about ten minutes they began to play.

Jaymi, who suffered from mild asthma, had found himself out of breath during the warmup and only managed to last twenty minutes into the game before falling to his knees.

The cold snow on his bare flesh soon had him on his feet again, and after catching his breath he continued to play.

Jaymi only continued for a few more minutes before stopping in his tracks. Michael, who had seen the first incident, went rushing over when he saw his friend bent double on the floor gasping for breath. Davies joined them shortly afterwards.

Michael handed Jaymi his inhaler which he had been carrying for him and after a few puffs on the inhaler Jaymi was able to stand upright. His breathing was almost back to normal and when he noticed everyone had stopped to watch, he was more embarrassed than anything.

Davies told Michael to go back with him to the main block to get changed and the two boys left the field together.

'Make sure you come back though Michael,' Davies called after. 'Just because your arm's broken doesn't mean you can't watch.'

They went back to the changing rooms, but Jaymi said he wanted to go back to the dorm for a bath. Michael picked up Jaymi's clothes and carried them draped over his broken arm as Jaymi puffed and panted his way across the schoolyard. They passed several sixth-form art students who were sketching the buildings, receiving the usual abuse that went on between the seniors and the juniors, though more so this time as one of the boys was the one who had been told off by the headmaster for refusing to post Michael's letter.

They finally reached their dorm and Michael put Jaymi's clothes down on the bed.

'I'd better get back before Davies sends out a search party,' Michael said, then added with more concern, 'Are you sure you'll be okay?'

'I'm fine,' he replied. 'It was more stitch than asthma.'

Michael left his friend undressing and made his way back to the sports field, stopping only to exchange a few foul words with the art students.

Jaymi ran the bath hot and deep - despite school rules - then lowered himself slowly into the water. He had become quite dirty whilst playing rugby but was in no hurry to wash. He had plenty of time for a long bath before showing his face back outside, so he decided to relax for a while. He closed his eyes and let the water cover his body so only his face was above the surface.

Martin sat in the car with the dog while Coles went into the police station.

'Won't be long,' he called over his shoulder.

Bradey was already at work on one of the phones when Coles walked in. He stood and waited for Bradey to finish.

'What was on the film?' Coles asked when Bradey hung up.

'Shit!' Bradey whispered. 'I forgot to get them developed.'

'You forgot?' Coles shook his head in disbelief. 'That's why I sent you back. What the hell were you doing all afternoon?'

Bradey explained that when he had come back to the station the Super had asked him to take a visiting high-ranking officer back to his office.

'Great!' Coles exclaimed. 'Did that take all day, or did you stay for tea?'

'No sir when I got back, I started to phone around some of the local banks. I thought I might get some information on Price's account.'

'Did you find anything out?'

'No sir. They refused to give any information over the phone.'

'Right!' Coles said. 'Where's the film?'

Bradey searched his jacket pockets and found the film where he had left it the previous day. He handed it to Coles, who handed it to the nearest constable.

'Take this to the lab and get it developed would you please,' Coles asked.

He then suggested they go to the banks in person before going on to the school, after all, the photos of Price and the money were the only clues they had and if Price had made a large withdrawal from his account recently, he might have something of interest to tell them.

Bradey took the list of banks from his desk, grabbed his jacket from the back of the chair, and followed Coles out to his car. Martin greeted them, then jumped into the back seat so Bradey could sit in the front.

'Got a new assistant, have you sir?' Bradey joked.

'God knows I need one,' Coles replied with rather less humour.

'Where to first Martin?' Coles asked his son. 'Lloyds or Barclays?'

'Lloyds!' came the enthusiastic reply.

Coles put the car in gear and drove off towards the bank. He was still in a good mood despite Bradey's incompetence.

Michael had only been back at the pitch for a couple of minutes when Mr Price came over to talk to Mr Davies.

'There's a phone call for you,' Price said when he considered Davies to be within hearing distance. 'It's about the anti-drugs meeting next week. I think they want to bring it forward.'

'Thank you,' Davies called back. 'Can you keep an eye on the boys?'

'Sorry, I can't, but I'm sure we can trust them for ten minutes,' Price said, looking over at the boys.

'If you're sure?' Davies questioned. He was not as trusting as his superior.

They left the field together and as soon as they were out of sight, the boys gathered together in groups and started to chat. Someone threw a snowball at Carl and soon the whole class were playing in the snow. It seemed Davies had the better judgement.

The fun in the snow was stopped by the sound of the school fire bell. Fire practice was a regular occurrence, and everyone knew the drill.

A buzz of noise came from the main building as chairs were pushed across the floor and boys piled down the stairwells, five abreast. Teachers shouted to gain control and within ten minutes the boys were outside, lined up in classes, having their names called by their tutors.

A few boys arrived late but Michael noticed Jaymi was not among them. He ran forward to where Mr Green, his tutor, stood.

'Sir! Jaymi's not here,' he babbled out.

'Shouldn't he have been with you last lesson?' Mr Green inquired.

'He was but he was sent back from games to get changed because of his asthma.'

Green finished calling the register for his class then walked with Michael to where the headmaster was standing.

'One of my boys is still in the building,' Green said. 'I'll go and see if I can find him. Michael knows where he was.'

'Okay. I'll keep the rest of them out here until you get back.'

Green and Michael walked off towards the second-year bathrooms in search of Jaymi. There must be a good explanation, it was so unlike Jaymi to break the rules.

Lloyds had turned out to be a dead end and so had Barclays. Coles and Bradey were waiting in the Midland for the manager to return when Martin walked in. He had been waiting in the car.

'There's someone calling you on the radio,' he said.

Coles told Bradey to wait for an answer, then went out to his car. He returned almost immediately with a great deal more haste.

'I've got to go to the school. Get an answer here then go to the rest if you have to. I'll meet you at the school later.' Coles turned on his heels and headed to the door with Martin.

'I haven't got a car,' Bradey called after them.

'Walk!' Came the reply.

ANALYSIS 8

Although I will focus this section on my Abingdon years, back in England, there is still no getting away from the influence Kent school had on my life. In my mind the St Philip's School of my fiction is Kent School in its entirety. As a result, the majority, though by definition then not all the scenes in the St Philip's story are drawn from my own experiences at Kent.

Rugby in the snow was definitely a Kent memory. I was actually on the school team for my age group and remember a particular trip out to an interschool competition. I have two distinct memories of the same incident. I was petite but fast so had been positioned as fly-half. The opposition were in possession and had broken through with some hefty lad - so hefty I wouldn't be surprised if he had been kept back a couple of years in school - steaming onwards for a certain try. Undeterred by his size I set after at pace and managed to catch him, launch myself into a glorious tackle, and bring his glory run to an end. Hurrah!

The second memory of the same event is as follows. The opposition were in possession and had broken through with some hefty lad - so hefty I wouldn't be surprised if he had been kept back a couple of years in school - steaming onwards for a certain try. Undeterred by his size I set after at pace and managed to catch him, launch myself into a glorious tackle, and bring his glory run to an end. Unfortunately, my tackle fell a little short and as my arms wrapped around his ankles, tripping him to the ground, his heel came up and caught me under the chin. I bit into my tongue, and although no serious damage was done, there was blood and swelling and I was unable to eat my pack lunch. I'm pretty sure mum had packed me a Cadbury Mini Roll that day too. Gutted!

The PE scene from the fiction serves a couple of purposes but I was pleased to read back that one of them is to return to the reason for Michael's broken arm. When this was referenced earlier in the story, I had a concern I had missed an opportunity but perhaps I was more organised than I gave myself credit for.

Although light on the elaboration of an experienced novelist, I am not too disappointed with the story I managed to weave. Okay, there are plenty of flaws and factual inaccuracies on police procedure, among other things I am sure, but there is also the thread of clues, hints, twists, and suspicions you would expect from a whodunnit. No Agatha Christie for certain but I may have scraped together something worthy of an episode of *Midsomer Murders* at least.

I do wonder if my positioning and posturing is creating any kind of suspense or if my story line and clue drops are a lot less subtle than I imagine. I am also reaching the conclusion Coles and Bradey may have been more than a little influenced by Colin Dexter's Morse and Lewis. Coles also displays traits that remind me of my father, but I used to think that about Inspector Morse too. Intelligent, Times crossword solver, condescending, arguably could have held a higher rank if he weren't so cantankerous, that kind of thing.

As I reread my ramblings in an attempt to keep the narrative flowing as intended, I realise I am being exceptionally honest on these pages. Honest about friends, about family, about work, and it is dawning on me that some of these people are quite likely to be reading this back at some stage if all goes well. I'm mostly okay with the thought of that but as our COVID return-to-work plans begin with three days back in the office from the beginning of April, I could do with getting this book finished and making my fortune.

More realistically I may need to revisit the preface and tone down a few elements to avoid being instantly dismissed from my job. I doubt I can count on the proceeds of this book to clear my mortgage and fund an early retirement, so I really should be mindful to avoid being sacked by disgruntled management.

Onwards to the Abingdon years. RAF Abingdon was situated on the outskirts of the town and this time our accommodation was off camp in a small military housing estate in the village of Shippon, Oxfordshire. Our allocated house was technically above my father's pay grade, usually reserved as an officer's quarter, but supply and demand resulted in us getting lucky, although not without some remedial RAF madness.

As an officer you are entitled to a few additional furnishings in your married quarters. I'm not sure what all the extras entail but the two specifics I recall were fitted carpets and a standard lamp. On our arrival these were still in place, however, the following week we received a correctional visit. The standard lamp was removed, fair enough, but beyond belief the sections of carpet in the living room that fitted into the alcoves either side of the fireplace were also removed. Two swift cuts with a Stanley knife and a bit of make do and mend and we were back to military standard with a rectangular piece of carpet, more than adequate for a Flight Sergeant.

With regard to other soft furnishings and our worldly possessions, a delivery of our packing boxes had already arrived from Germany while we were staying short-term in the accommodation block. My father had been over in advance of us to receive them and then travelled back on a return trip to accompany us home.

We always travelled light so many of my toys were binned or given away to friends to avoid the need to pack too much. I expect there was an allowance of boxes we had to stay within, at least I hope so otherwise it was a bit harsh to deprive me of my whole Action Man collection at the age of twelve.

There was excitement to come though. Before we moved to Germany my parents had decided to put the majority of our belongings into storage and that storage container was being delivered back to us during the first week in our new house. Perhaps I should have said amusement rather than excitement, four years is a long time for tastes to change when it spans the late seventies and early eighties.

I am fairly sure we travelled back during the Easter holidays of 1983, facing rearwards on a less than glamorous military aircraft, so I was starting my new school mid-year. I wasn't too daunted, although it's never great navigating your way through the first few days and weeks of being the new kid. 'What's your name... where you from... Oooo! Say something in German.'

The other thing I noticed pretty quickly was how different an English comprehensive school was compared to the overseas English-speaking school I had come from. I soon adapted after being mocked for calling the teachers Sir or Ma'am when responding to a question in class. I don't think Fitzharrys was even a particularly bad example. Abingdon is in rural Oxfordshire, not some inner-city, but the rules and discipline were much more lenient than at Kent.

The other new observation for me was the bullying. I am sure there was a degree of bullying at Kent, but I never saw it. I guess at Kent the students were from a lot narrower section of society, the majority were from military families with parents who were used to certain levels of discipline themselves. Whatever the reason, I did not intend to become a victim.

On my first day, in a lesson I can't recall, I had been sat next to one boy who insisted on jabbing my arm with a pencil, testing the boundaries with the new boy I assume. Later in the lesson, when the teacher was addressing the class and all were quietly listening, I noticed he was rocking on the back two legs of his chair. I turned and caught his stare and, with a discreet flick of my foot, kicked the chair from under him sending him crashing noisily to the floor. As he was reprimanded by the teacher, I offered out my hand to help him up. At the subsequent break time some other boys seemed shocked I had taken him on, but I never had any further issues with him.

With a potentially more serious group off bullies it took a little more perseverance to orchestrate their desist. This group were clearly the ones to watch in our year and would go on to be involved in some serious incidents in the years to come. As usual there was a leader and his entourage of three lackeys. They used to give me a little bit of grief during breaks, again the new boy is an obvious target, but nothing too serious just a bit jibing and pushing around, but it was becoming quite regular and laughing it off was not working.

One of the lackeys happened to be in my class and as we waited to go in, he started to tug on either my hood or my backpack, I don't remember which. I am not sure if he had forgotten he didn't have his backup crew with him, or if he was becoming overly confident with the threat level he possessed, but I took my chance. When he tugged at me yet again, I spun around and pushed him into the wall behind him and grabbed my hand around his throat. I swear I lifted him off the ground a little, and he looked genuinely scared.

'You and your fucking friends leave me alone, and I'll leave you alone!'

That was all I said before I let go. I have no idea how his own conversations played out with his gang mates, but they were never a problem for me again. This was not, however, an act of vigilantism aimed at correcting their ways. All I was interested in was taking myself out of the line of fire. They continued to be a problem for others and as I mentioned, things only escalated.

A rather awkward lad who was a bit of a loner had attracted their attention and one day after school, while he was trying to escape their chasing, he rode his bicycle out into the road and was hit and killed by a car right outside the front gates of the school. Later still, I believe two of them were expelled for their involvement in some form of sexual assault on another student. Maybe 'escalated' was a bit of an understatement for the migration from hood-pulling to rape and murder? Alleged of course, I am not in possession of all the facts for these events, and I am sure the cycling incident was classed as a tragic accident. The playground chatter said different though.

Not wishing to make light of what were serious events, but for me it wasn't all bad at Fitzharrys. I enjoyed my time at the school and again made my separate collection of in-school and out-of-school friends. My main partner in crime when not at school was Simon and we kicked about together most days, drifting apart a little towards the end. He is another person that fell by the wayside when I moved but we reconnected on Facebook years later with a few messages of hello, but no relationship was ever rekindled.

Back then though we were inseparable for the best part of three years. The eighties were great, so many things were changing. Breakfast television launched with TV-am, Channel 4 had already launched a year earlier giving us four TV channels to choose from. Yes, four! The pound coin came into circulation, Cadbury launched the Wispa with a mysterious star-studded advertising campaign. BandAid followed by LiveAid gripped us, and in the last year before I moved away the space shuttle Challenger exploded live on television.

Throughout all this we were developing as adolescents too. We were starting to buy music and take more interest in clothes and haircuts, not that either of us were any kind of trail blazing trend-setter; we were computer buffs. Clive Sinclair, before diving down the rabbit hole that was the C5, had launched the Spectrum computer and myself and Simon had bagged one each for Christmas. We would spend our pocket money and spare time fighting through the levels of *Jet-Pac*, *Manic Minor*, *Jet Set Willy* and many more titles.

For my thirteenth birthday I had also received a portable television for my bedroom. We had *Max Headroom*, *The Young Ones*, *V*, *Only Fools & Horses*, *Auf Wiedersehen Pet*, *Spitting Image*, *Miami Vice*, and many more which were all essential viewing for playground banter the following day. And the cinema never let down an '80s child either. *E.T.*, *The NeverEnding Story*, *Beverly Hills Cop*, *Back to the Future*, *Top Gun*, *Gremlins*, *Big*, *Police Academy*, *Splash*, *Lethal Weapon*, *Indiana Jones*, *Stand by Me*, *Empire of the Sun*, and *The Goonies* for crying out loud! The frickin' Goonies!!!

The school trip to Kilvrough Manor happened when I was at Fitzharrys but I have talked about that so I will tell you about something else that happened for the first time in Abingdon instead. I reconnected with a friend, Michael Oram, my wheelbarrow race partner from the Silver Jubilee.

Michael was not actually in Abingdon but after moving back from Germany my parents had gotten back in touch with a couple of their friends from a previous posting in West Drayton. They were now living in Weston-Super-Mare and were also friends with Michael's parents who lived there too. My sisters had been friends with this couples' daughters, as well as Michael's sister, and we were all going down to visit.

It was a bit of an awkward first encounter walking around a park in Weston, as we had only been nine the last time we met and were now fourteen, but we soon hit it off again. For years to come we would be pen pals and when we learned to drive, we began to meet up. Michael would go on to be the best man at my wedding and remains my longest friend to this day. He will feature again through these writings so I will come back to it all in due course.

Michael was the friend regained during the Abingdon years, and although I also lost touch with Simon, I very much felt Darren was the friend I lost here. I've already covered in some detail this brief encounter but to position it in time, it occurred in the six months prior to my leaving Abingdon, when my closeness to Simon was waning.

There was no great fall out between us, I think we were just growing into different people with different interests. I also knew we were going to be moving away with much more notice than normal, as my parents were finally buying a house in our next destination, so perhaps there was an element of self-preservation, knowing the inevitable was coming and we would soon be parted.

Frustratingly there really was no need for me to be parted from my friends on this occasion as we were only going to be moving fifteen miles away but despite my protests, by way of teenage sulking, there was to be no compromise. I had finished my O-level exams at Fitzharrys, and we would be moving during the summer holiday, and I would be starting Sixth Form at another new school. This was by far the worst move yet. I truly believe it impacted my further education and changed the course of my life. Not that I am unhappy with where my life has gone, but it was certainly an emotional trauma at the time.

The only other afterword on our Abingdon departure references back to the RAF rules, regulations, and consequential inefficiencies. The back garden of our house was lined on its boundaries by substantial six-foot-high hedges. Not long before we moved away a team of people came along and trimmed these all neatly back into shape. Shortly afterwards, another team of workers came along and ripped them from the ground and replaced them with wooden fence panels. Not to worry, at least they had managed to recover the cost of my father's missing egg spoon all those years ago.

CHAPTER 9

Coles skidded to a stop outside the school then stepped from his car. He was greeted by a young constable and Mr Price. They explained what had happened as they led the way to the bathroom where Michael and Mr Green had found Jaymi's body. Martin started to follow but Coles suggested he take the dog for a walk instead.

Jaymi's naked body was still in the bath when they arrived. His eyes were closed, and he looked as if he would wake any minute and ask what was going on. His protruding knees were still dirty from rugby, but through the water you could see the rest of his body was clean and white. He looked so pure and peaceful. He reminded Coles of his own son when he watched him sleeping, as he often did.

The cause of Jaymi's death had been electrocution and the source, a tape recorder, still lay in the water beside his head.

Coles examined the scene, in his mind trying to find a connection between Jaymi's death and the murder of McWinney. This was, of course, impossible for him to do simply because he had no idea why McWinney was killed, let alone young Jaymi Lowman. Much as he hated to do so, he had to admit it did look like an accident.

Jaymi was having a bath. He had been listening to his stereo when it had fallen into the water beside him. The building was old and surely the inquest would ask why there was a power socket in such close proximity, but these things happen, it was believable, but to Coles the coincidence was just too much.

When Cleaps arrived he too could only suggest an accident as cause of death until it was proven otherwise. There were no signs of a struggle except for some water on the floor, which could easily have been splashed as Jaymi's body convulsed from the shock, and there were no other visual signs to suggest any other cause of death.

Cleaps promised Coles he would contact him immediately if the post-mortem revealed anything out of the ordinary. He also confirmed that McWinney had hit his head on the window frame as he fell. The blood sample had been fresh, and the type matched.

Coles decided he was really going to have to get to work on this case if he ever hoped to solve it. The only lead he had was the money and the photographs. Bradey was looking into the money side, so that left the pictures. He considered confronting Price but decided to wait and see if Bradey had found anything out first. Instead, he decided to take a look at the photography rooms. It seemed a reasonable assumption that the pictures had been developed on the premises, so it was worth a try.

He had asked for directions and was on his way when Bradey arrived back from the bank.

'You were quick,' Coles greeted.

'His account was at the Midland,' Bradey explained. 'The manager came out with the details just after you left.'

'What did you find out?'

'He has a joint account with his wife. His wages are paid directly in by the school. All his bills are paid by direct debit and there has only been one large withdrawal which was paid straight into a trust account in his grandson's name.'

'Excellent!' Coles exclaimed.

'What next sir?'

'I was off to the photography rooms but now you're here we may as well go and see Price about these pictures.'

'Right!' Bradey nodded, then followed Coles as he led the way to Price's office.

They waited with Price's secretary until he was ready to see them. He buzzed through on the intercom as soon as he had finished on the phone, and Julie gave them the nod to go through. Bradey held open the door as Coles walked through, fumbling in his inside pocket for the envelope containing the photographs.

Price greeted them with a firm handshake, then motioned for them to take a seat. They did so, but first Coles leant over the desk and placed the envelope on the table in front of him.

'What can you tell us about these? We found them amongst Mr McWinney's personal belongings.' Coles sat back in his chair awaiting the response.

Price took a seat, then began to study the pictures one by one with great interest. He flicked through them again and again. After a few minutes Price cleared his throat with a cough then spoke.

'Why would he have these pictures of me?'

Coles explained that the photos had been found with a great deal of money, and he suspected McWinney had been blackmailing him.

'What! That's absurd, I've never paid the man a penny for anything,' Price's voice was louder now. 'And what would he be blackmailing me about? These are just pictures of me walking down the street. I was out drinking with a friend.'

'What would your friends name be sir?' Bradey asked. He had his pen and paper ready for the answer.

'Tony Westman. He's a teacher at the college. I've got his number if you want it, but it's in the book.'

'I'll just take it down if you don't mind,' Bradey said, leaning forward to see Price's address book.

When Bradey had finished, Coles stood up to leave. He took back the photos from Price and flicked through them himself.

'Are you aware that the pub in the background of these pictures is a homosexual establishment?'

'No! And if you were wondering, we weren't in it anyway, we were just walking past,' Price snapped.

Bradey had just one more question before he put his pad away.

'How often do you see Mr Westman?'

'Most Fridays. We go to lunch together.'

Bradey put away his pad, then he and Coles thanked Price for his time and left. They headed for Coles' original destination, the photography rooms.

As soon as he was sure they had gone, Price picked up the phone and began to dial. The call was answered after only three rings by the college receptionist.

'Witney College, how can I help you?'

Price asked to speak to Tony Westman, and the woman on the other end put him through to his extension.

The phone rang twice more before being answered.

'Hello!'

'Tony? It's Ken.'

'Hi, what can I do you for?'

'The police have been asking questions. They've got photos of us together. I told them we meet on Fridays, but not at the club. If they get in touch with you tell them we go to the Jubilee on the High Street.'

'Sure,' Tony said, his voice more serious now. 'Perhaps we had better not meet this week.'

'No, that would look suspicious. We'll meet at the same time as usual but in the Jubilee instead. Just in case they check on us.'

'Fine. I'll see you there then,' Tony said, then hung up.

ANALYSIS 9

We are a little over halfway through the original story now and we have arrived nicely at the second body you would expect in any reputable crime drama. I thought I might have dwelled a little more on this scene, I feel the reveal should have been more emotional perhaps. Maybe on the screen it would be more powerful than on the page, seeing a dead child's body revealed in the water, or perhaps I am just not very good at writing, or wasn't then, or both. It also occurs to me now that a body electrocuted to death in the bath may not just be laying there looking serene and angelic, as if still asleep.

You have had enough information now to be drawing some conclusions. There are clues here and previously that could even enable you to establish if this death were indeed accidental or suspicious and, spoiler alert, to also arrive at the motive. Maybe you already have, maybe I have been much less subtle than I realise.

Mr Price is clearly back under suspicion but is he too obvious a suspect? They always try and lead you off the scent by throwing you a prime candidate. Or maybe it's a double bluff, it can't be him because it's too obvious, but it actually is him after all. Also, I have introduced a little homosexual angle to proceedings with attention being drawn to the gay bar in the photo. This would not have been mainstream for an eighties television drama if that is where my aim was, perhaps my forward thinking was due to the barrage of AIDS adverts in the eighties. That may have sparked the idea, maybe it was something else.

Martin is also now conveniently in place at the school for his part in the unfolding events, or more accurately his dog Boss is in place. I also reference Witney here, which is the town where I attended sixth form. The Jubilee pub referenced also existed in the real world and was in the village of Bampton where my parents had purchased their first house, and still live to this day. This day being 1st April 2021, my first week back in the office as UK lockdown restrictions begin to be lifted again. For legal reasons I am obviously writing this during my lunch breaks and in the evenings or weekends, certainly on my own time.

The house in Bampton was an old married quarter which had been sold off by the RAF at a generously reduced price. The logic was fifty percent below market value, but I think the market value had also risen since the price had been set so my parents managed to get a three-bedroom end terrace for £25,000.

There were around fifty homes available in this sale and you could view and select your preferred three before being

entered into a selection process based around years of service, rank maybe, I'm not entirely sure. My father was successful and was allocated his second choice I believe. I had
the third bedroom, it was tiny, half the size of my previous
one in Abingdon. Could things get any worse with this
move?

Of course they could. Bampton was a small Oxfordshire
village, filled with Morris Dancers, Aunt Sally players and
inbreds. Some ticked all three boxes I am certain. Bob
Monkhouse told a joke about an Oxfordshire village he had
moved to where he had met a local man out walking with
his wife and sister. There was only one woman with him.
You get the picture.

In reality, it is a lovely village, but I didn't want to be
there. That's not to say there isn't some truth in my character assassination, I find stereotypes are based in some element of fact, and Bampton was years away from being the
tourist destination it would become through its use as a film-
ing location for *Downton Abbey*.

With echoes of the bullying in Fitzharrys, a few locals
had decided the new boy needed to be initiated into the village. I was out one evening with some friends I had made at
school, who weren't in my classes of course, and one of the
locals punched me in the head. There were a few newbies
who had arrived together, and some came off worse than
others. I didn't make much fuss and it all blew over pretty
quickly.

This was all happening within the first week of arrival
and just a few days later I got myself caught up in another
incident at Witney Feast, the local fair which came to town
each year on the second Monday of September. A group of

us had just ridden the Waltzer and as we stepped off, I stumbled and bumped into a young couple. I knocked the girl's hot dog into her coat and made a small amount of mess. Turns out her boyfriend was one of the Bampton boys who had a reputation for being a bit thuggish. My new friend Ian knew them and calmed the situation, but he was in no doubt there would be repercussions back in the village at some point.

Corrina was a girl I knew in Abingdon, whose parents had also bought a house in Bampton at the same time as my parents. As we had arrived in Bampton together and clearly had some shared history, I can only assume this led to us being confused for brother and sister. When the boy from the fairground had been enquiring to plan his reprisal, some mistaken local must have told him he had been bumped into by Corrina's brother.

I heard he had arrived at their house and told Corrina to get her brother outside as he was 'gonna smack him', or something to that effect. Corrina did in fact have a brother, Kerry, who was deaf but much more importantly was three years older than me and much bigger. On being told someone had come to fight him, he marched outside, smacked three shades out of the stranger in his garden and sent him on his way. I was never bothered again by that guy either.

Ian, who had de-escalated the fairground incident, had become a good friend very quickly. We travelled from Bampton to Witney on the school bus together each day and spent most evenings and weekends together along with a small group of others. I was taking A-levels and Ian was resitting some O-levels so again we did not share classes. Actually, we did share one, he must have been taking an AS level science class as well.

In the evenings we would likely be wandering the streets of Bampton or sitting in the playpark as teenagers like to do, a little bit of knock-and-run on occasion but we weren't really a mischievous bunch. Ian was also an Oxford United fan and I got into the routine of joining him for the home games at their old Manor Ground stadium, although I wasn't really a football fan. We also used to travel down to London on occasion, on the newly launched Oxford Tube bus service. Our little gang trekking around Oxford Street and Carnaby Street, feeling all grown up at the grand old age of sixteen/seventeen.

Ironically, this friendship came to an end pretty abruptly after only a year when Ian moved away, albeit not very far, and he also left sixth form after completing his re-sit exams. His parents were not in the forces, but they had decided to buy a house out of Bampton. I visited there, and Ian slept over at mine one football Saturday, and we also met up at lunchtimes in Witney too when I was still in sixth form and Ian had started a management training scheme in Waitrose.

These meet ups stopped completely shortly afterwards and all of the above contributed but there was another major factor I will come back to, one of those sliding door moments that could have changed the course of my life completely. As it was, Ian is another friend I have never met again since.

Around this time, my life did change quite significantly in several ways. I had lost interest in further education, predominantly because all the friends I had made at Henry Box Sixth Form were taking re-sits and left halfway through my A-level courses. I told my parents I didn't want to continue, which would have been a disappointment to them, but I softened the blow by showing an interest in joining the RAF instead.

I took a summer job in a warehouse in Witney while I went through the RAF recruitment process and would end up working for that company, Floridan, for ten years - starting my IT career loading paper into printers and changing ink cartridges. The RAF thing didn't really work out for me. I had set my heart on a particular career working as an aircraft and engines engineer, but colour blindness ruled me out from that particular role. I had passed the entrance exams and other roles were available to me but I had lost interest a little now and I had money coming in from my employment so there was no rush.

I also considered the military and the civilian police. Much to my mother's dismay one of the recruitment officers who came to discuss this with me at our home arrived in a marked police car and parked it on our driveway. What must the neighbours have thought?

The police force wasn't for me either, time passed, and I stayed put at Floridan. Not a bad decision with hindsight, as it was the foundation for my career to date which has contained reasonable achievements and financial rewards over the years, despite me now feeling somewhat artistically frustrated again and hence the renewed writing endeavour. Or is this just a standard mid-life crisis?

The departure of Ian from my life left a hole in my evenings and weekends and these became filled with Sian. She lived on the same estate as me, RAF parents who had purchased like my parents, but she attended a boarding school near Bristol. It was the summer holidays and she had been hanging around with our little gang but now it went further, and I had asked her out. The gang was all but disbanded and life was now all about having a girlfriend.

I couldn't yet drive but a friend from work had passed his test and he took me down to Bristol to visit Sian at her school one weekend, I think on the promise that he might have an opportunity with her friend Jane. Our relationship grew stronger, and we would be together for around three years. We lost our virginity together, we had a pregnancy scare as the result of a broken condom, and we also got engaged. We were too young really, but our parents supported us, and we had an engagement meal by way of celebration.

Sian's vocation in life would turn out to be nursing and she began this career studying as a trainee nurse when we were together. This would in fact be the start of the end for us. She was living away in nursing accommodation at the old Princess Margaret hospital in Swindon, and although I could now drive, we saw much less of each other, and she had her own social life and new circle of friends.

I heard a rumour through a mutual friend that she was becoming very friendly with a guy called Lee. Enraged, I headed over to Swindon to confront her. As I waited in her accommodation for her shift to finish, I noticed she had a calendar on her wall and the week on display was blocked out in capital letters '- - L E E - -'. I couldn't believe it; she was clearly having a week off with him.

Now this should be a heart-breaking story, and at the time I guess it was. Sian was seeing Lee and wanted to see him more and we did break up over this. What is funny is the story of the calendar. When she came back into the room after her shift, I began my rant and pointed out the indisputable evidence on the wall. Sian proceeded to page through her calendar and show me that every week was filled with a different combination of dashes, L's, and E's. These signified her shift pattern of lates, earlies and days off. Ooops! We did get back together briefly after this, but it wasn't the same and before long we amicably arrived at the decision to split for good.

While I am reminiscing about some of the downs in my life, let me introduce the subject of my testicles, or one of them at least. As with a lot of my stories, and my general approach in life, I can find humour in the darkest of moments. This certainly started off as a dark moment, but there was light at the end of the story, quite literarily.

I was eighteen, working in Witney, and getting towards the end of my time together with Sian when I had noticed a lump on my right testicle. I was not the embarrassed type who would dwell on an issue until it became more of a problem, so I took myself off to the GP in Bampton. This is how I recall the events of the following week.

The Bampton GP ran an open clinic on a Monday which you could go along to without an appointment. I went along but the Monday clinic was run by a nurse, and when I explained my ailment, she made me an appointment to come back and see the doctor. On the Wednesday, the doctor had a little fumble around in my pants and was concerned enough to get me an appointment at the Churchill hospital in Oxford. On Thursday, my father turned up at the warehouse I was working in, which was very unusual. He had received a phone call to say the Churchill hospital appointment was on the Friday and I would likely be staying in for surgery.

On the Friday I had an ultrasound on my scrotum and then a doctor explained that there was a tumour on my testicle, and his recommended course of action was to remove the offending testicle the next day. They would then perform a biopsy and if the tumour proved cancerous, I would start a course of radiotherapy. This would almost certainly leave me infertile so I would be invited to leave a sperm donation prior to this treatment for later use, should I decide to start a family.

Being eighteen, I was over the age of consent, so all this took place without anyone else being present. My father had dropped me off at the hospital and four days later, lighter by one testicle, my sister picked me up to take me back home and await the biopsy results. I think I had a phone call, but no visitors.

Roughly a week later I had a phone call to tell me the biopsy had shown the tumour was benign and no further treatment was required, other than a trip to the GP to have my wound checked. As quickly as it had happened it was all over again. I can only imagine if this same scenario happened nowadays there would be more support, regardless of the biopsy outcome. In roughly a fortnight I had gone from healthy, to dying, to healthy again or at least that is how it felt in my mind. I dealt with it, I'm good at that.

A year later I went back to the GP as I had been informed it was possible to have an implant for aesthetic purposes - not that I was in the habit of flashing my testicles around. The procedure only required day surgery so while I was there, I got them to throw in a circumcision too! Joking aside, I did also get circumcised. I had been noticing a little discomfort since being sexually active and I knew my father had a similar issue in his teens. Turns out they cocked that up, so to speak, and I actually ended up getting re-circumcised a few years later too.

As a side note, I am still in contact with Sian on occasion and interestingly her nursing career has led her to specialising in urology, the field of medicine which covered my intimate dramas. Coincidence maybe, subconscious bias, or maybe she just likes willies.

The light at the end of this tale of genitalia woe is that I somehow discovered that if I push a torch into the back of my scrotum, my implanted testicle glows in the dark. It's quite a party trick and also works with the torch on an iPhone so can be displayed quite spontaneously. My disco bollock is well known amongst my circle of friends.

CHAPTER 10

The photography department occupied a small area in one of the art rooms. The dark room was to the rear of the class, and the light above the door showed it was unoccupied.

To one side of the room there was a filing cabinet. It contained the pupil's work. Each boy had a separate drawer to store his pictures in, and Coles was impressed by some of the work as he flicked through. He was looking for a file on McWinney.

As a member of staff McWinney was entitled to use the school facilities and did so. Coles found a drawer with his name on it.

The file contained several high-quality prints of buildings, animals, people, and a variety of other subjects. Many of the pictures were taken through special lenses and it was obvious McWinney had been no amateur.

As good as the photos were, there was nothing of interest to Coles. He was not sure what he was looking for, but this was clearly not it. He replaced McWinney's work and continued to search the room.

After a short time, they had worked their way along the length of the room, leaving only the dark room unsearched. They both went in, switching the light above the door to red as they did so.

The dark room was typically small and very tidy, thanks to the strictness of the teacher. This made it far easier for them to search.

Bradey recalled a film in which a detective had found a photo upside down in the water tray used when developing. The white back of the picture was hidden against the white of the tray. Bradey succeeded only in wetting his fingers, while Coles mocked him.

'I saw that one too,' he laughed.

Bradey smiled back as he wiped his hand on his trousers. For the next few minutes, they searched in silence. Coles checked the cupboards under the work surface, whilst Bradey examined the pictures that had been hung to dry on a piece of string that ran between two nails in the wall. One of the pictures was pegged the wrong way around, and as Bradey unclipped it to take a look another fell from its peg and went down behind a bookcase.

'What have you done now?' Coles asked, lifting his head from one of the cupboards.

'I knocked a photo down behind the bookcase,' Bradey admitted.

Coles stood up from his squatting position on the floor and went over to help Bradey move the bookcase away from the wall. He wondered why there was a bookcase in the dark room, but on closer examination he saw the books were mainly on nude art photography. He presumed they were

in there to stop the younger children from giggling over them when they had an art lesson in
the room next door.

As the bookcase came away from the wall Bradey
could see there were three pictures behind it,
and not just the one he had dislodged. Two of
the prints were just typical exam pieces, but
the third was of McWinney swapping parcels with
a man in a back street neither Bradey nor Coles
recognised.

'Well, well, what do we have here? Seems
McWinney might have been a naughty boy,' Bradey
said with a certain satisfaction at having found
the picture.

Coles took the photo and examined it closer.

'Drugs? he asked Bradey.

'Could be,' Bradey replied. 'Or blackmail?'

From the picture it was impossible to tell
what may or may not have been in the parcels,
but there was definitely something suspicious
about the swap, and the photo.

'I think we should go back to McWinney's rooms
and see if we can find something we may have
overlooked the first time,' Coles suggested.

Bradey nodded and after replacing the bookcase they left the dark room and began to trek
across the school again towards McWinney's
apartment.

Martin was running alongside Boss. They
turned the corner by the outside sports changing
rooms and found themselves about ten yards away
from a group of boys. To Martin they looked
about fifteen and were bullying a younger boy
of about eleven.

Boss had stopped a few paces ahead of Martin
and was now growling at the mob. They turned to
see Martin and his dog. One of the boys threw a
stick at Boss, which he had previously been

stabbing into the boy's crotch, and Boss re-
treated whimpering. Martin never whimpered, but
he did run. His sense of civic duty was not yet
strong enough to override his instinct of self-
preservation.

The previous victim was left, to his relief,
and the crowd chased after Martin like a pack
of hunt dogs fresh on the scent.

Martin ran faster than he had ever ran before. The length of the main building had flown
by, and he was just rounding the corner down to
the main drive. The group chasing him had no
chance of catching up so had stopped trying, but
Martin was unaware of this and just kept running. A look of relief came over his face when
he saw Bradey and his father halfway down the
drive. He stopped running but walked quickly to
catch them up.

Coles asked what the rush was, but Martin
just told him he had been racing the dog, which
now stood by Bradey's side.

Martin decided it would be best for him if he
stayed with his father for a while, so all three
of them continued on the journey to McWinney's
rooms.

Only one constable now stood guard. He recognised Coles and unlocked the door as they approached.

The place was the same as they had left it
the day before, and Coles stood quietly looking
around.

'There must be something we've missed,' he
said, breaking the silence.

Martin and Bradey waited for Coles to continue, but he didn't. The silence returned. Boss
walked around the room sniffing the air and Martin had visions of him cocking his leg against
a chair and taking a piss on it.

Suddenly the silence was broken once again, though this time not by Coles but Boss. He was barking and tearing at one of the cushions from the couch.

Bradey tried to take the cushion away from him but was snarled at when he approached. Coles received the same response and only Martin could pull the dog away.

Coles examined the cushion, and as he removed the cover several small plastic bags fell to the floor. He picked it up and guessed that the substance contained within was some form of drug, which would later be confirmed by the lab boys back at the station. Boss barked again and pulled at his lead in an attempt to get to the package. Martin silenced him with one quick tug.

'Well now!' Coles grinned. For the first time he felt he was making progress with the case. 'I guess we'll have to get you a big bone tonight,' he said to Boss.

They walked outside and Coles ordered the officer on the door to seal the room again. He turned to Martin.

'I think you're going to have to go home now son, I'm sorry.'

He half expected Martin to flare up as soon as he finished his sentence.

'That's okay, I understand,' he replied.

Coles explained to Bradey that he was going to take Martin home.

'I want you to get this place searched by sniffer dogs, then go and have a look around. If McWinney was selling, then someone must have been buying,' Coles said. 'See if there are any kids with withdrawal symptoms or something. I won't be long.'

Bradey walked off to use the phone, and Coles, Martin and Boss headed towards the car.

ANALYSIS 10

Rather convenient that the school caretaker was a keen photographer who developed his films onsite but from my limited experience I don't feel it unreasonable to use convenient coincidence in a whodunnit, they certainly did in the *Murder, She Wrote* style dramas of my youth.

With hindsight I would probably have given the detectives more reason to search the school dark room. Perhaps when they had found the original photos in McWinney's rooms I should have specified they were on oversized paper, leading to suspicion they had been self-developed.

There is also a link back to my friend Ian here as when we were at sixth form together I recall going to the Henry Box School dark room with him. My memory fails me if it was actually Ian studying photography or another of our friends, but we definitely had cause to be there at some point.

You'll have spotted this is where my conspiring to get Martin and his dog to the school delivers its payoff. Before the main event there is the little run in with the school bullies, which I could easily claim is a nod to the bullying experiences of my own youth, but I suspect it was just another attempt to pad out a chapter. It's all about the word count, I can't tell you how often I am word-counting this new rendition in the hope I am going to be able to spin it into an acceptable size for publication.

I suspect we may not hear from Martin or Boss the dog again now they have served their purpose in allowing the plot to evolve just a little bit further. I seem to have been very clinical with my prose, with almost every scene and event being of relevance to the developing plot.

I also note, no crime is really being solved here. Events are just being observed as they unfold. Despite my naivety of due police process and procedure I suspect this element of my story telling is much truer to life than any master sleuth, such as the great Poirot or Holmes, single-handedly solving some Machiavellian chain of events.

In my personal life we have now made it to the end of the eighties. I started the decade moving back from Germany, in the full throes of puberty, and proceeded to lose some more friends, my virginity, a fiancée, a testicle and my foreskin, but towards the end of the decade I gained a driving licence, a job, and some money in my pocket to burn.

Being able to drive enabled me to reconnect with Michael in person rather than just as the pen pal he had been for a number of years. I would visit him at his parents' home in Weston-Super-Mare and we would go out and get very drunk on bottled K-cider, and he would also make return trips up to Bampton.

On one of the occasions he visited, we took ourselves off on a road trip back to West Drayton where we had first met. I drove there in my trusty Austin Maestro, and we were so excited to be going back. Things started to become familiar as we neared our estate, passing the old RAF camp and the parade of shops we used to go past every day on the school walk.

We parked up and had a good look around, we walked the walk back to our old primary school and it was great, it was nostalgic, it brought back good memories. We talked about things we had long forgotten but that the familiarity of the surroundings had re-triggered. The Silver Jubilee, obviously, other friends we had known, the episode of *Some Mothers Do 'Ave 'Um* filmed at Mulberry Parade. It was called the *Psychiatrist* and resulted in poor Frank Spencer being buried in sand just in front of the shops we would walk by every day.

And then there was the time Michael chopped my finger off. I would say that sounds much more dramatic than it was, but I would be wrong. We were around seven years old and had been playing in Michael's back garden. For some reason I had climbed on top of the wrought iron garden gate and when Michael proceeded to open it, the top of my finger was trapped in the hinge and severed through the first joint of the finger.

There were screams and a lot of blood. Before I knew it, I was sitting on my mother's lap in the passenger seat of our car, finger wrapped in a towel, as my father drove us to the hospital. The top of the finger accompanied us, luckily still attached by a thread of skin.

The only other thing I remember was crying to the doctor as he said I was going to need to have a little operation to reattach it and that meant I was going to miss *Dr Who*. Home video recorders were yet to be invented and this was a very traumatic thought. Strangely, and please remember my sceptic personality, my father had a similar injury to the same finger at the same age. Spooky!

Along with the freedom of mobility my car gave me, I also had the income from my first job, which by the early nineties I had been working at for almost three years following my fizzled out attempt to join the RAF. Still living at home and paying only a token amount for housekeeping left plenty of money for the weekends, which would usually consist of drinking locally in one of the many public houses Bampton had on offer.

When I first moved to Bampton there were eight pubs in the village. I believe at one point there had been twelve but over the years this has only continued to dwindle, and I believe there are now only four remaining, possibly even three, we shall see in the coming weeks which ones emerge from lockdown. It is April 12th this coming Monday, and Boris has decreed we can return to public houses as part of our COVID exit plan, although only in beer gardens. It is to be another five weeks before we are allowed inside, and then another five weeks later before we are back to the 'new normal', whatever that means.

Drinking in Bampton was fun, I had a new group of friends there following the Sian split, and I played darts and pool and even occasionally got dragged into a game of Aunt Sally. Witney was the local town though, and nights out there with work friends were becoming more frequent. Witney had a nightclub, The Palace, housed in an old cinema building and that was the place to be, there or Sidings, another club which had an old railway carriage as the entrance to the building. I remember many a night bopping away to the B52s *Love Shack* before throwing up, which was a regular occurrence at the end of my evenings out.

Maybe for this reason I was not having much success on the romance front on my nights out, but this was about to change. Not as a result of any improvement in my drinking or dancing skills, but through an introduction to a girl at work. Not even a girl, this was a fully grown woman. I was twenty and working in the warehouse, but it seems I was attracting the attention of Jill from Finance, age twenty-seven no less.

I guess you would say we courted a bit, chatted at work as we got to know each other a little more, and then I invited her to a barbecue at my sister's house, happening around about my twenty-first birthday. I know Jill was extremely nervous meeting some of my family, but it all went well, lubricated with alcohol as all our family events were.

We went out at weekends together and as well as going to The Palace, Jill introduced me to Witney Football Club, which was an interesting night out I had not previously experienced. Before long I started to spend the night at Jill's house in Witney, rather than having to head back home to Bampton, and our relationship was consummated. To the album *Introducing the Hardline According to Terence Trent D'Arby* I seem to recall, and one testicle or not I was in my prime, I could go twice before Terence finished his 47 minute 11 second accompaniment!

My parents hadn't been at the barbecue so had yet to meet Jill, but they were aware I was seeing someone and spending some weekends there. I remember one afternoon asking my mother if I could use the phone to call Jill and as I did so my mother hovered in the kitchen making a cup of tea. The phone rang a few times and then a little voice answered. 'Hello, can I speak to your Mum,' I said to Hayley, Jill's four-year-old daughter. I swear I literally saw my mother's ears twitch and her eyebrows raise.

When I got off the phone my Mum subtly began her questioning. She hadn't realised Jill had a child. Oh yes, I told her, she's twenty-seven and divorced too. Oh, the alarm in her voice, I was dating a divorcee with a child. This was almost as bad as when the police had parked outside the house. I exaggerate a little and it was all fine. My parents met Jill shortly afterwards and before long I had moved out of their home and moved in with Jill, still only twenty-one and now a live-in partner and kind of father figure to Hayley I suppose.

Hayley was a beautiful little girl and is now a beautiful young woman. She is thirty-five, married to Ben, is herself now a stepparent to Ben's teenage son Neo, and has a daughter of her own, Ronni, who I very much consider my granddaughter. Only last week I visited them all in their new home, just a forty-minute drive away. Ronni is practically a clone of her Hayley at the same age.

One of my abiding memories of Hayley in the early years was sitting with her as she was learning to read. She would bring home a book from school, one of the ones with the same sentence on every page, bar one word. John likes to go to the park… John likes to go to the shops… John likes to go to the zoo… John likes to go to the cinema… You get the idea. The frustration as she would read everything perfectly and then on the last page say something completely different as if every word had changed. We joke about this still, especially as she has now experienced the same thing with her own daughter.

As I mentioned, I initially moved into Jill's rented house, but we soon decided to buy a house together. In fact, before my twenty-third birthday, we would have bought our own home, got married and had our son, Aaron.

Money was not in surplus during our early years together. I only earned a warehouse operatives wage, Jill had changed to part-time working following the birth of Aaron, mortgage interest rates were high, and although we had managed to clear the help to buy part of our initial mortgage deal, there was never much money left at the end of the month.

Our wedding was a small affair at Witney registry office, with Michael as my best man, followed by a meal at a local hotel. Jill's wedding dress was made by a friend, I had a suit from Burtons, and the honeymoon was a few nights away at a friend's mother's B&B in Woolacombe, which was lovely but would have been lovelier in the summer.

We were married on 6th February 1993, a little earlier than planned when we had discovered Jill was pregnant, and Woolacombe hadn't really awoken from the winter at that point. On our first morning there I ran across the road to see what time one of the little shops opened and the sign on the door informed me it opened in April.

Things did get easier though. I was getting on well at work and had a few promotions and pay rises, eventually moving into the offices and beginning my IT career. Interest rates started to fall and house prices started to rise. I had also taken a weekend job working at a local bookmaker, the owner of which would go on to be shot dead on his doorstep in some love triangle or another, but for now there was little extra cash coming in for socialising, although we tended to do this separately, with the other looking after the kids so we didn't have to pay for a babysitter.

We would suffer a very worrying but luckily brief setback when the company we were both working for went into administration. The company was saved from administration and relocated from Witney to Swindon. Not great as we now needed to commute but at least we remained employed.

Six months later the company folded although we were both retained by the administrator to assist with the wind down so our salary was protected, and we even received a small bonus on top of our redundancy payment. We both found new jobs straight away so the whole sorry affair bizarrely left us with some savings for the first time. We had a lovely little porch added to the front of our house in fact.

We spent around nine years in that house as a young family and I have great memories, although there are also photo's that are not so great. I am sure those clothes and that decor seemed much more fashionable at the time. Nothing wrong with a young father and his son having matching nineties undercut haircuts is there?

There were frantic Christmas' trying to find the must-have present that always seems to be sold out, I remember a Dipsy Teletubby and Buzz Lightyear specifically. There were birthday parties and barbecues and everything you would expect. We had saved for a new kitchen, and we had a couple of UK summer holidays to Dawlish Warren and

Weymouth. We even managed to afford our first summer holiday abroad with my parents to Son Bou, Minorca.

And before you know it the best part of a decade has passed, and we are into a new century no less. I made another little bonus working in IT at the turn of the century as there was genuine panic that computers around the world would crash when the two-digit year turned from '99 to '00. The world survived and I happily banked the money.

We were on the up, and we decided to move house. Not very far at all, maybe only five-hundred yards as the crow flies, but it was on a nicer estate and was a four-bedroom detached house. It needed some work, and another new kitchen, but it was a lovely house. We hadn't quite risen to the heights of an ensuite, but we were certainly now in with the downstairs loo crowd.

Although not superstitious at all, I am intrigued by life's little coincidences. Two more have occurred to me while writing this chapter covering my time in Witney. I have recently watched *The Pembrokeshire Murders* on television, one of the highlight dramas of lockdown. Halfway through, I realised I recognised the story and indeed one of the couples murdered while on holiday in Wales, Peter & Gwenda Dixon, had been from Witney. I remember them going missing and the discovery of their bodies back in 1989.

To add to that, the soundtrack of the program included the choral song *Suo Gan*, which had also featured in one of my favourite movies, *Empire of the Sun*, released in 1987 when I was just starting the St Philip's story and choir music was a central theme.

The other event that stuck with me from the years in Witney with Jill was Princess Diana's death. Tearfully watching the funeral cortege with the two young princes walking slowly behind her coffin, supported by their grandfather, Prince Philip. Yesterday, at the age of ninety-nine, Prince Philip passed away. As I type these words, I can hear the shots ring out of the forty-one-gun salute being covered by the news channel in the background.

Isn't life strange. The twist and turns, the memories, the coincidences, the repetition. Life is circular, everything still to come is linked to everything that's gone before. Maybe.

CHAPTER 11

Martin made no fuss as he stepped from the car outside of the house. He donned a false smile and waved to his father as he reversed down the drive and pulled away. Martin wished he could have stayed at the school, but really could understand why he had to come home.

Coles decided to go via the police station on his way back to St Philip's. He had a few things he needed to sort out, and he hoped that the film would have been developed.

At the station he was greeted with the usual grunts from his colleagues, though one of them managed a whole sentence.

'The photo's you wanted are on your desk, sir.'

Coles nodded his appreciation then went to his office to collect them.

He opened the packet and flicked through. He stopped, turned back a few, then removed one of the snaps and put it to the top of the pile. He examined the picture more closely, then flicked through the others he had missed, being careful to leave the selected print on the top of the pile.

'Well, well!' he exclaimed aloud, then replaced the pictures in their pouch. He handed in the packets of drugs found in McWinney's room to the nearest officer and asked him to deal with them. The other jobs he had planned to do could wait. He was in too much of a hurry to return to the school and confront Price with the latest photographs.

Bradey had supervised the start of the search in McWinney's rooms, then left to see what else he could find out. He was at present, in the sick quarters waiting to speak to the registered nurse. He only had a short wait before she joined him.

Bradey asked if there had been any boys in to see her recently with sickness and fever, then asked to see them when she explained there had been, and they were still with her. She led him through a door at the back of her office into a six-bed dormitory made up to resemble a hospital ward. The three beds to the left were empty but the three to the right each housed a sick-looking boy.

Bradey went to each bed in turn. He pulled the curtains around the bed for a little privacy then whispered his questions. He spent little time with the first two boys as they rightly or wrongly claimed ignorance to his line of questioning, insisting they were simply feeling unwell. He had much more success with the final boy, Dominic.

After spending quite some time with Dominic, Bradey left the ward. He thanked the nurse on the way through her office then went off in search of one of the female officers working at the school. He had extracted the vital information from Dominic but thought a female officer might put him more at ease while he made a full statement. With any luck the other two boys would be able to add something as well.

Bradey had just given the constable her instructions when Coles arrived. He showed Bradey the photos, and they began to walk towards Mr Price's office once more.

'Did you find anything out?' Coles inquired.

'I went to the sick bay,' he started, 'there were three lads in there with bad fevers. I put a few suggestions forward about McWinney and drugs. Two denied all knowledge, though I'm not convinced, but the third admitted taking something and he said he bought it from McWinney.'

'Good work, is someone taking a statement?'

'Constable Harris has just gone to see them, I thought they might find it easier to talk to a woman.'

Coles was satisfied that things were coming together quite well and was sure that Price would be able to provide a few of the missing links.

Coles pushed open the door to Price's office with some force. They had walked past Julie without waiting to be announced, and Price was startled by the unexpected intrusion.

'Can I help you?' Price asked, outwardly calm.

'I don't like people who fuck me around! Sit down and explain this!' said Coles, clearly angry.

Price took a seat and picked up the photo's Coles had just thrown on the desk in front of him. He swallowed hard as he saw the first picture, the one Coles had deliberately left to the top.

Coles spoke again before Price had a chance to.

'You told us you had never been in that bar, yet the photo shows you coming out of it with Tony Westman. Are you having a homosexual affair with him? Was McWinney blackmailing you about it? Did you kill him because of it?' Coles' voice was raising with every word.

'No! Well, I mean yes.' Price paused to compose himself. 'I am seeing Tony, but McWinney never approached me about it. As far as I was aware nobody knew about us, and nobody can. I'm married you see, with a son and grandson. It would ruin me.'

'Perhaps you should have thought of that before you got involved.' Coles had no sympathy for people who obstructed his investigation. 'You are now our prime suspect. Do not leave this building - not that you'll be allowed anyway. I just hope this is the full story this time.'

Coles left the office and Bradey followed. They stopped further down the corridor to talk.

'That should have put the wind up him a bit,' Coles said, now completely calm again.

'Don't you think we should have taken him in, sir?'

'No. I want to speak to the boy and teacher who found Jaymi's body in the bath. There has to be a link, and until we find a few more links we don't have enough for a case against Price anyway.'

They walked on in search of Michael. So far so good, but there was still some way to go before any conclusions could be drawn.

Coles and Bradey entered the back of the church. They had asked one of the boys outside if he had seen Michael, and almost without thinking the church was where he suggested they try.

Colin Sheppard, the choir master, came over to them as they stood in silence and awe admiring the aged architecture and ornamentation, as soft choir music drifted on the air causing them to almost forget why they had come in.

'Can I help you gentlemen?' Colin spoke softly, attracting their attention.

'Pie Jesu. Is that the school choir?' Coles asked.

'Yes. They're quite good, don't you agree?'

'I always find it difficult with choir music to make out the words,' Coles admitted.

'You should think of their voices as another musical instrument. The notes they are playing are not so important, it's the overall sound that matters.'

'I'm sure the lyricist would beg to differ.'

'Perhaps you would like to come to our Christmas concert on Saturday? Tickets are available by donation. It has become somewhat of a tribute concert to Jaymi.' Colin's mood changed visibly. 'He was a fine chorister.'

Before Coles could refuse, Colin had taken two tickets from his pocket and handed them to him. Coles, in return, took some money from his wallet and paid a guilt-inflated donation.

'We just wanted to have a few words with Michael Bracher,' Bradey added to the conversation, eager to get away before he too was invited to part with some money.

'He's just down the front,' Colin directed. 'He's been in here for a couple of hours. Pie Jesu was one of Jaymi's favourite solos and Michael keeps asking me to play it for him. He

179

just sits and listens. I think his heart is broken.'

They thanked each other before Coles and Bradey walked to the front of the church to where Michael sat.

Michael's eyes were red from crying, and for a while he found it hard to speak. He had been in the church practically the whole time since he had found his friends' body in the bath. Price had suggested they arrange for his parents to come and pick him up from school, but Michael didn't want to go. He had spoken to his mother on the phone and explained that he just wanted some time to himself, and they should pick him up at the end of term, as planned, on Sunday.

Coles could understand how Michael was feeling and was silent for a while as he tried to think of a tactful way to ask him the things he needed to know, the way he would have liked to have been asked when his wife and daughter had died. He was about to speak when Michael started to talk. He was looking straight ahead as he spoke.

'He was murdered you know, Jaymi,' Michael said. 'I saw him. Mr Price did it.'

Coles was taken aback. 'You were outside when it happened, you couldn't have seen him,' Coles pointed out, but Michael wasn't listening.

'But he didn't know about the radio. Jaymi knew. You knew, you were there,' Michael continued.

'He didn't know what about the radio?'

'It was broken. When you came to see us in our dorm Carl knocked it off the bed. It hasn't worked since.'

'But you couldn't have seen Mr Price put it in the bath, you were outside.'

'No, you don't understand. I saw Mr Price upstairs yesterday. He must have thought I was Jaymi and killed him instead of me.'

'Why? What did you see him do upstairs?' Coles asked, excited but more than a little confused.

'Nothing, but I saw him go into the room Mr McWinney fell from just before it happened. He must have known someone was watching him. It should have been me.'

Coles looked over to Bradey. He was writing in his note pad but lifted his head as Coles looked over. They could see from each other's expressions the surprise and excitement Michael's statement was bringing.

'It's not your fault Michael. Don't think that.' Coles put his arm around Michael's shoulders in an attempt to offer comfort. 'Why didn't you tell me you were upstairs when I spoke to you in the hall?'

'I shouldn't have been up there, it's out of bounds.' Michael bowed his head.

'Nobody would have been cross,' Coles said. He did not want to push too far in case he made Michael feel any more guilty about his friend's death.

'I couldn't tell you. I was doing something private with myself. I didn't want anyone to know.' The tears began to flow once more. 'Jaymi's dead because I needed a wank!'

'It's not your fault,' Coles repeated, feeling choked himself. 'You've told us now and nobody needs to know why you were there, that can be just between us.'

Coles held Michael in silence until his tears had slowed, then left him in the care of Mr Sheppard. Coles explained to Michael that he would have to send someone over to take a statement, and that he would have to tell them what happened, except for their secret, so they could write it down. Michael nodded, seemingly calmer now he had unburdened himself, then Coles and Bradey left the church.

'I don't think we need to speak to the teacher who was with him, do you?' Coles asked Bradey.

'Nope, let's just get Price in for questioning,' Bradey replied.

'Agreed! But first...' Coles had noticed Constable Harris up ahead, obviously finished taking statements from the boys in the sick bay.

Coles briefly explained that he wanted her to take a statement from Michael. He warned her that he was upset and insisted she did not ask him why he was upstairs when he reached that part of the story.

When fully instructed, Harris made her way to the church and Coles and Bradey to Price's office yet again, though this time when they left, Price was with them, and wearing a nice pair of matching bracelets.

ANALYSIS 11

As a seventeen-year-old boy I was clearly a little naive as to the ins and outs of drug use. I am still not all that worldly-wise, but it seems a little unlikely that schoolboy recreational use would have invoked withdrawal requiring medical attention within the twenty-four hours so far elapsed in the St Philip's timeline. As with most of the detail of the story, it was there to meet the need of my narrative, factual accuracy was secondary at best, absent often.

Likewise, I am sure the police would not be interviewing schoolboys without a parent or guardian present, although it was the eighties, so the world hadn't yet entered the realms of political correctness gone mad. I must have drawn my understanding from somewhere, likely influenced by my boyhood television diet. I'm pretty sure Regan & Carter would have just got on with it.

I am more impressed by my plot planning, namely the broken stereo being planted quite early in the story for later use in the death of Jaymi. Hopefully, it was subtle enough that you didn't spot it until Michael pointed it out during his teary ramblings. I don't recall having planned ahead in quite that way, I thought I had almost made the plot up as I went along but obviously I had done a little preparation, a straw man of a plot that I had then weaved around. And we are not quite done yet, there is a little more still to be revealed.

The other element of this chapter I like is the utter, inconsolable, devastation Michael is feeling at the loss of his friend, and indeed his part in the circumstances surrounding it. It is another example of a scene I would love to be played out on screen. I am aware my writing is almost certainly too weak to translate the emotion I envisaged in my mind, on to the page.

A teenage boy crying is such a powerful thing to see. One such scene that sticks with me is from the movie *Stand By Me*. River Phoenix' character, Chris Chambers, is recalling the tale of when he was accused of stealing the milk money. He breaks down in front of his friend Gordie in a mess of tears and snot bubbles. It is very powerful on screen, I don't think even the great Stephen King captured that level of emotion on the page in his novella, *The Body*, on which the film is based. I quoted from the book earlier in this tale. Both the book and the movie had a profound impact on me back then, as did River's untimely death.

If you were to ask my friends or family if I were an emotional person, I suspect they would say not. They would be wrong. I have a tough exterior and I portray myself a certain way, for my own reasons, but I am actually extremely sensitive. The turn of the century was to bring me some very tough times to deal with, and I would be crying snot bubbles of my own on a number of occasions during the next decade.

We had probably been in our new home for a year when my sister asked me to pop around to her house for a chat. She lived within walking distance, and it wasn't a particularly odd request as we did see each other quite often, so off I popped, unconcerned. Not one to mince her words, within the first few sips of a bottled beer she had handed me, my sister was informing me that she had been told that Jill, my wife of ten years now, was seeing someone else.

A little taken aback, I asked for some clarity. Apparently, it was a guy Jill worked with and she had most recently been out with him only this previous weekend, not just with him in fact, but in a foursome for a meal with her brother and his partner.

It seemed plausible as Jill had gone out the previous weekend, with the girls I had thought, and I had stayed home with the kids. I finished my beer and left. My head was spinning, I would be home in five minutes and would have to confront Jill, but I decided to call her brother first on the walk home.

Andrew's partner Julie answered his mobile as he was driving - they are married now but I don't think they were at the time. I very coldly asked what she could tell me about this guy, I won't name him as he is definitely one of the people who falls into my unworthy of note category, even Jill would now label him so.

There was an element of fluster from the start and as I elaborated and said I understood they had all been out for lovely meal recently, Julie said she would get Andrew to call me back shortly. Her voice had already confirmed it was true though. No need, I told her, I would be home in two minutes, and I would ask Jill myself.

When I walked in the door the telephone was ringing. Jill was just about to pick it up but before she did, I managed to say, 'That will be your brother'. She looked a bit puzzled as I walked away and waited in the kitchen. It was her brother, and the cat was out of the bag. After a short conversation with him she came through to where I was waiting and that was the start of the end of our marriage. I was angry and upset and there was never any question in my mind whether we should attempt to work through this issue, and I don't recall Jill wanting to try either. We were getting divorced.

Jill moved into the spare room, which only seemed fair as I had not done anything wrong. We spoke to the kids about it, which was difficult, but we were aligned and said all the right things, it was never acrimonious. We began divorce proceedings with our respective solicitors, which would also go relatively smoothly, with an amicable financial settlement and never any doubt there would be joint residency of the children.

The only thing I regret is that I agreed to accept unreasonable grounds on my part as the reason for the divorce, to speed up proceedings. I should have stuck to my principles, it was adultery. With hindsight it doesn't really matter, I suppose, anyone who knows us now makes a completely different assumption about the reason for our divorce anyway, but we will get to that.

The house would need to be sold but we hadn't been there very long, so we weren't giving up a sentimental family home, although in the last twelve months I had hung and glossed eleven new doors so that was a little heart-breaking.

Joking aside, what would happen in the next couple of months, as we worked this all out, would truly leave me hurting, physically in pain, as I cried it out alone.

It started out quite unexpectedly from my point of view. Jill was going to be renting a new house for her and the kids, and I would remain put until our house was sold. I would then end up staying with a friend while I made another purchase. The thing I wasn't expecting is that Jill wanted to get into her new house, decorate and order furniture and get everything all sorted out before the kids moved in. The result was Jill moved out and the kids stayed with me, and I had a good number of weeks as a single father.

This period was great. I was making the lunch boxes and doing all the washing and school runs and Sunday roasts, the whole kit and caboodle. I could imagine it was very hard for Jill, although she was still coming around and seeing the kids obviously, and I would realise just how hard it was when it all came to an end.

The dreaded day came. Jill was ready for the kids, and I was going to drive them over with the final bits of their belongings and then they would be living with her full time, visiting me at weekends. I prolonged the drop-off by having a drink and was shown around the house. It was looking good, and the kids had a few new things, so they were excited about the whole thing, but it wasn't long until I had to say goodbye.

Now I know people get divorced all the time, and I know kids are resilient, and I know it can almost be better being the weekend parent because you get to do all the good stuff and not the nagging about tidying rooms and doing homework. All of that is true and looking back everything has worked out well for me, certainly better than it did for Jill in the early days of her new relationship, but in that moment when I had to walk away and leave Hayley and Aaron behind, I could barely speak.

There were hugs and then I walked away to my car. I was crying before I got the door open and I barely stopped until the house sale completed and I could finally get out of the shell of our old home that I was now bouncing around in on my own, the kids' rooms stripped bare of any sign they had ever been there. Even when you are a rational thinker and you know things will all work out, in that moment it feels like bereavement, and it hurts.

The decree absolute came through in August 2004, by which time I was living in my new house in Carterton, only five miles away from the kids, and everything had settled into a new routine. I had taken Aaron on holiday to Cyprus with my best man Michael and his son, and life was looking up again. I wasn't quite ready to get back to dating again, but it was coming, and I will focus on that in the next chapter.

Of course, just when the relationship disaster of the first half of the decade had come to an end and things seemed to be improving, life likes to throw another challenge at you and so I will finish this part of the story talking about my son, Aaron, before circling back to my next relationship adventures.

Aaron was born on 13th July 1993, just six days before my own twenty-third birthday. Not a completely planned pregnancy but we were engaged to be married and contraception was clearly not a fulltime commitment for either of us.

After informing my parents of the pregnancy and being congratulated by my father that my genitals still actually worked after their medical history, we decided to pull the wedding forward, hence our wintery February honeymoon.

The pregnancy was uncomplicated, a bouncing baby boy arrived three days after his due date, and that was our little family complete, Me, Jill, Hayley, and Aaron.

Finances were tough but we survived, and things improved over time. No great dramas through childhood, he was an early speaker, an early walker, cute as a button and he would go on to make friends easily and do well at primary school and on into secondary school.

Upset obviously, but Aaron took the divorce in his stride, and when we come to the part about my next relationship, he took this in his stride as well at an age when it all could have been quite stressful. But something else was going on for Aaron, something he didn't share until very late on in his suffering, and it was going to be life changing.

As best I can recall, my first knowledge there was a serious problem was when Jill rang me to say Aaron had called her from school in a bit of distress. By distress, I mean he was sixteen years old and was calling from the toilet to ask his mum to come and pick him up because he had shit himself, no longer able to control his bowels.

Aaron had been having some issues, losing a little weight and some toilet trouble, but we had no idea what he had been putting up with. He had medication from his GP, although we suspect he wasn't taking it as prescribed due to an aversion to swallowing tablets, but following this incident things escalated fast.

I really could not be clear on the exact timings or sequence of events that followed but needless to say it was rapid and something along these lines. A trip back to his GP, a referral to the hospital specialist which, thanks to my work health insurance, came through very quickly at a private hospital. There was the need for an investigative colonoscopy, and this had to be halted during the procedure due to the doctor's concern at the severity of Aaron's condition.

The diagnosis was severe ulcerative colitis, Aaron needed to be transferred across to the main surgical hospital as they would better be able to monitor him there. He was to have his large bowel surgically removed and would have an ileostomy resulting in a stoma bag.

This was a lot to take in. It was all happening very rapidly, as with my own cancer scare when I had been just a little older than Aaron was now, another little echo of the past repeating. The whole time Aaron's health was deteriorating, dropping to a dangerously low weight as a result of what was effectively malnutrition. The side-effects were described to me by one nurse as similar to anorexia. He was on all sorts of drips and supplements to try and regain some balance to his chemistry, but the surgery was going to be required urgently.

The day of the surgery was awful, one of the most sickening days of my life. Aaron was taken down to surgery around lunchtime and I waited at the hospital with Jill, and we waited and waited. Updates were few and far between, and the time just kept passing until eventually someone came to see us in the waiting room later that evening. He announced himself as the surgeon and my head dropped, I am not naturally pessimistic, but I was certain he had come in to tell us Aaron had passed away in theatre.

The surgery had gone well, although a little more complicated than it could have been, and Aaron was back in recovery, and they would be bringing him up to the ward in the next hour or so. We were warned he wouldn't be very responsive, and he had a few tubes and wires about him.

When we were taken back to his bedside it was a shocking sight, every hole in his body had a tube in it, and they had made a few extra holes besides. He was intubated, had a catheter, cannula, anal drain, abdominal drain, with electrical pads still attached to his chest and the little peg thing on his finger. He was unconscious on pain relief and when we left him there to go home for some sleep, I was still petrified he might not make it through the night.

I am pleased to say he did make it, and actually recovered pretty quickly. I think he had been feeling so ill, for so long, that having a stoma bag put him in a much better place than he had been. He started to gain weight and we soon got into a routine of less and less frequent check-ups, moving finally to just an annual review.

Once the threat of death had passed, we also found humour in it, as we do with most things. Aaron very much has his father's sense of humour. He was in a band, and he liked to joke that he didn't even have to leave the stage for a poo during a gig, but he was getting older, and girlfriends were something that changed his thinking on the stoma situation.

The stoma nurse had explained there were vanity pouches you could put on which are much more discreet for short periods of intimate time, nobody likes a bag of shit banging their forehead when they are trying to give a blowjob, I think I may have joked, but Aaron had decided he wanted to go for a reversal operation.

The whole process had been explained in the early stages of his recovery as a possibility for the future. It was not a required operation, and many people choose to live with the stoma as there are other risks involved with the reversal process. One of these risks, which was explained again during the pre-operation consultancy, was impotence. The operation requires deep pelvic invasion and there is a not insignificant risk of nerve damage which can result in full and permanent impotence.

He would need to donate sperm prior to surgery for future fatherhood should things go wrong, yet another echo of my own past, but Aaron decided he still wanted to have the operation and he was now above the age of consent, so it was fully his own choice to make, although I would have supported his decision had he required me to. So, he was back in hospital, and we were going through all that stress again.

It was much more straight forward this time as he was much healthier for this surgery. Recovery took a little while as the surgery was a two-stage process requiring the new anal pouch to heal before they could perform a second smaller operation to reconnect it and remove the secondary stoma. The nail-biting part was in the first forty-eight hours after surgery, waiting for anaesthetic and pain relief to subside so we could see if impotence had been avoided.

Aaron happily announced he had popped a boner one visiting time, so all was good. It is easy to joke now, I dread to think how he may have coped had something gone wrong and he had been impotent from the age of nineteen.

You would think that might be enough for someone to cope with in one lifetime but only in the last month Aaron, now age twenty-seven, has been back to hospital again following a short period of weight loss and further pain. This time he has been diagnosed with Crohn's which they have managed to control with injections it looks likely he will have to take, every fortnight, for the rest of his life.

I want to just add for public record that Aaron has never really moaned about any of it, and I am so proud of my son and will take this moment to tell him so, and that I truly love him. I am fully aware I am a little too like my own father, so I definitely never say this enough, not to Aaron, or Hayley, or any of the other people I care about in my life. I'm sure you all know who you are, I love you all, very much.

CHAPTER 12

Price was left alone in the interview room for a short time while Coles considered his line of questioning. All kinds of ideas raced through his mind but in the end, he decided to just play it by ear.

Bradey came to join him, with a packet of tapes for the recorder in the room, and together they walked in to confront Price. There was silence as Bradey loaded the tape recorder, then Coles started the ball rolling with his standard entrance, stolen from some film he could no longer remember.

'I've already told you I don't like being fucked with, so every goddamn word from here on in better be gospel or your ass is grass and I'm a lawn mower.'

'I don't know what you mean, I've told you everything I know,' Price answered, unintimidated.

'Bollocks! I've got a witness who saw you going into the room McWinney fell from minutes before it happened. Now would you like to start again, we've got all night.'

'Nothing happened, I swear. McWinney must have found out about Tony and decided to black-mail me. He asked me to meet him in one of the old classrooms on the top floor, so I did. He showed me the first set of photos you had, and said he wanted money.'

'Is that when you pushed him through the window?' Bradey asked.

'No! I didn't do it. I denied his allegations. The pictures showed nothing incriminating so I refused to pay. I guess I was calling his bluff. He never mentioned the second set of pictures, and I figured that if we were careful, he could never prove anything.'

'So, what happened?'

'I just left him there. I went back down to my office, and when I arrived Andrew was with Julie, and they were calling an ambulance.'

Price appeared to be telling the truth, but who could tell?

Coles was about to ask his next question when there was a knock at the door and a young officer entered. Coles announced the interruption to the tape then begged an explanation from the officer.

'Could I have a word outside sir?'

Coles and Bradey stepped out of the room and the young officer explained himself.

Whilst searching Mr Price's office one of the policemen had found a partially burned letter in the fireplace. The edges were singed, but the main text was still legible. It was a letter to someone called Richard. It had only been signed 'Me at school', but as Coles read through it seemed obvious who had penned it.

The letter told of how the sender had seen someone go into the room from which McWinney had fallen. Price's name was not mentioned, but the letter read pretty much the same as Michael's statement.

'Interesting,' Coles said, after finishing the letter.

'What is, sir?' Bradey inquired.

'Well, it all fits together very nicely. Price kills McWinney, then he somehow comes across this letter exposing a witness, so he kills him too. The only problem is that Michael was the witness and Jaymi is the one that's dead. Surely if you were going to kill someone, you'd make sure you had the right someone!'

'Maybe Jaymi wrote the letter. Michael could have told him what he had seen and Jaymi might have just been retelling it,' Bradey suggested.

'No. The letter is in the first person. I'm certain Michael wrote it, but why the mix up?'

'Mistake?' Bradey offered.

'Bloody big mistake. We'll have to talk to Michael again and find out if he did write the letter, and if he did, we need to know why the killer thought it was Jaymi. Anyway, I don't want Price to know about the letter just yet. There's a few more question to ask first.'

Coles thanked the constable for the information and told him he would keep hold of the letter for now. Bradey went to get three cups of coffee from the machine, and while he was gone Cleaps walked past Coles in the corridor. Coles called to attract his attention.

'Any news on the Lowman incident?'

Cleaps looked over his shoulder, then walked over on seeing Coles.

'Nothing of interest to report,' he said. 'Cause of death was electrocution. No other damage to the body, and I heard about your drug bust but I'm afraid this one was as pure as he looked when you saw him in the tub.'

Coles thanked Cleaps for the update then returned to the interview room. He said nothing until Bradey returned with the drinks.

'What can you tell me about your schools' drug problem?' Coles began.

'Well,' Price started. 'There was an overdose some time ago, a boy called Stuart Walton I believe, I'm sure there's a tree with his name on it somewhere. Surely you don't think I had anything to do with that. I've only been at the school for five years and it must be nearly ten since he died.'

Coles took Bradey to one side of the room. 'Check out that story, and I want to know about any other drug incidents at the school,' Coles whispered, then announced aloud Bradey's exit from the room before continuing his questioning.

'What I should have said was, what do you know about the current drug problem at St Philip's?' Coles corrected himself.

'What problem?' Price was confused.

'We have reason to believe McWinney was selling drugs to some of the pupils. Since his death, several people have shown mild withdrawal symptoms, and we found a quantity of an illegal substance in McWinney's quarters.'

'Then he deserved his comeuppance,' Price stated with conviction.

'But that wasn't your decision to make,' Coles fired back.

'Nor was it a decision I made. I didn't kill him, and I know nothing about the drugs.'

Price seemed genuinely surprised to hear of the drug situation within his school, though Coles had decided to doubt all that Price said without substantiation.

'That's all the questions I have for now,' Coles said.

'Does that mean I am free to leave?' Price asked. 'Because on the subject of drugs, there's an 'Anti-drugs In Sport' meeting I am expected to attend.'

'Where would that be?' Coles asked out of interest.

'It's at the school. Mr Davies is chairing it, and I said I would be there. He's into all that kind of thing, and it's St Philip's turn to play host. Ironic I suppose.'

'There is paperwork to complete and be signed, but after that you will be free to leave.'

Coles stood up to leave the room. He stopped at the door, turned around, and in his best Columbo voice said:

'Just one more thing, sir.'

'Yes?' Price asked.

'Do you teach any of the boys at the school, or are you just the headmaster?'

'Oh, I teach as well. Just the lower-school boys, but I think that qualifies.'

'What about Jaymi Lowman?'

'Yes!' Price smiled as he spoke. 'I remember him well. He used to write funny little poems and I would sometimes read them out in class to keep the kids amused. Such a waste of a life, and just before Christmas.'

'Thank you,' Coles finished then left the room.

Bradey was in the computer room reading through printouts. When Coles arrived, he began to reread the important parts of the text out loud.

The printout confirmed the death of a boy named Stuart Walton, eight years ago, and had details of the following investigation. The man who had supplied the boy with drugs had been caught and prosecuted on several charges including child abuse. He had died under suspicious circumstances whilst serving his sentence. There had been no other reported drug incidents at the school since then, and Coles showed little interest in the information he had just been given. He was more concerned with the letter which had been found in Price's office.

'Bradey, I'm going home, but first thing tomorrow we must check out this letter. I don't think Price is our man. I want you to let him go, but not until you get a man to the school to discreetly guard Michael. I'll explain it all in the morning.' Coles started to walk away.

'What shall I do with this printout?' Bradey called after him.

'File it!' Coles shouted back over his shoulder and then was gone.

ANALYSIS 12

For me, this chapter is another example of some inexperience in my writing, combined with a television fuelled understanding of police interview techniques, which I hope is acceptable at seventeen. I clearly had a good cop/bad cop idea in my head, although I notice Bradey never gets a chance to be the good cop. Speech writing is difficult though, or I find it so at least, perhaps when I move on to my next writing venture I will try and craft an idea that contains as little as possible, or maybe even take a creative writing course.

With regard to the 'your ass is grass' quote Coles uses in his opening gambit, I cannot recall which movie I would have heard this in. I have done a bit of Googling, but nothing is really striking a chord, except to say that it originally seems to have been credited to a 1956 Tab Hunter movie called *The Girl He Left Behind*. This is another one of those quite bizarre coincidences in life, two-fold on this occasion, and I will reference it again shortly in this same analysis section.

What else? Oh yes, the partially burned letter found in the previously unmentioned fireplace. I'm generally pleased about this little plot thread, like the tape recorder sewn very early on in the story if you spotted it, but I do now appreciate the missed opportunity to elaborate on my descriptive writing. An office in an old school building with an open fireplace would have been the perfect subject for descriptive prose and would have set the scene for when the burnt letter was later discovered.

Coles is putting the pieces together nicely. Michael's unsigned letter discussing an unnamed suspect who had been seen on the top floor entering the room the body had fallen from. But if that suspect saw Michael, why was it Jaymi who was killed? Not to forget Mr Davies being mentioned as a big anti-drug advocate, and we already know that he had to leave the playing field during the PE lesson to take a phone call at roughly the same time Jaymi went off to the bathroom. Still, not all the pieces are in place, but we are getting there.

The name Stuart Walton is bothering me, I feel I should remember the name, but I don't. I have mentioned before all the names in my fiction had an origin from some friend, acquaintance, or event in my life but this one is escaping me. It's quite likely two people, I have been doing a bit of mix and matching with Christian and surnames but still I can't pinpoint this one. If it comes back to me, I will let you know, and if you are Stuart Walton and are offended by my memory loss, I apologise.

Okay, so back to real life. I think it is fair to say that most people who know me would probably describe me as a nice person, with a caustic sense of humour, and probably a little cold to the touch. Although I recognise this in myself, I do not believe it to be the whole truth. I am not as heartless as I may appear at first glance. The noughties, as a decade, definitely hardened me with the experiences I have described. All of which came on top of my own teenage health scares, but it only hardened the shell. I am still a big softie underneath and people get glimpses occasionally.

This softer side exposed itself quite dramatically mid-2000s, about a year or so after the divorce from Jill, and before Aaron was taken ill with ulcerative colitis. This was the period when I came out as a gay man.

Not that being gay makes you soft per se, but I certainly stressed, deliberated, and cried a whole lot while I went through this life-changer in my head, playing out scenarios about how friends, family, and most stressful of all, how my children might react.

Before I get into the detail let me just address a couple of previous references I said I would come back to. Most recently I referenced Tab Hunter as the original source of the quote Coles used when questioning Mr Price. For those unaware, Tab Hunter was a major Hollywood heartthrob actor who later came out as a gay man. When I wrote the St Philip's story, I had no idea who Tab Hunter was, so it is a complete coincidence that I used this quote when Coles is questioning Price about his sexuality. In addition, it falls into the spooky coincidence category and reflects a little on my own coming out, although if I had given it some conscious thought the signs were there. My childhood was quite fluid with regard to who I was willing to play doctors and nurses with.

The second point goes back to the divorce. As you can imagine it is now widely assumed our marriage ended as a result of my homosexuality. This is not the case. Jill was completely unaware of the feelings I was having, and they were absolutely never acted upon, however, I am prepared to accept the mere fact that my head was racing with these thoughts might have had some bearing on how good of a husband I was. It doesn't matter now anyway, and Jill was amazingly supportive throughout the whole process, a process that went a little like this…

The divorce hit me hard, and I had been single for well over a year and it was approaching Christmas 2004. For a few months I had been considering the future and I already knew that my next partner would be a man, I just couldn't imagine anything else. It was pre-Grindr days, thankfully, but there were plenty of websites you could explore your feelings on and chat to people. Gaydar and Ladslads spring to mind but I am sure I frequented other sites as well.

I owned a webcam and it was used, I cannot deny, but mostly I chatted to people, for hours sometimes, and to this day I still occasional have contact through social media with some of the people I met during those times.

Unlike Grindr, which lets you know your nearest gay is only 100m away, in the good old days the geo-locational stuff was not really a thing. This meant you could be chatting to people from all over the country - even the world - if you wanted, but I tried to keep focused on the UK. I was thinking of getting back on the wagon relationship-wise ultimately, so it seemed a little impractical chatting to someone too far afield.

When you have been chatting to the same person for some time, and you have shared interests and are seemingly getting on well, it is only a matter of time before one or the other of you suggests you should meet up. Then before you know it you are heading down to Southampton to meet your online friend for dinner, with an invitation to stay the night, but you've both agreed you'll see how dinner goes before that commitment is fully made. It wasn't too long a drive down from Oxfordshire but long enough for me to be getting extremely nervous about our meet up, nervousness that required alcohol to calm, therefore, I would not be driving home that night.

Luckily, dinner went really well, and we were both enjoying our evening. Either before or after, we walked the streets a little and I remember the Christmas market, and a block of flats being pointed out that apparently Craig David had lived in and written his debut album, *Born To Do It*, in his bedroom.

Inevitably we ended up back at Marcus' house, extending the evening with a couple more drinks while listening to music, but eventually the time came to go to bed. There was a spare room, it was offered out of politeness, but we both knew it was going to remain unused that evening. I was nervous but I wanted to experience another man so badly, teenage fumbling aside, this was my first time. I can safely say I was not as born to do it as Mr Craig David himself, but I certainly enjoyed myself and Marcus was very understanding of my inexperience.

The postcoital doubt was a killer though. I was awake the whole rest of the night with thoughts racing through my head. I just wanted to go home, maybe there is something to be said for a Grindr hook-up after all, where you just cum and go, so to speak.

Morning eventually arrived and it was okay, not too awkward. We spent the morning together and went for a walk around a park or nature reserve of some description before I said my goodbyes and got back on the road. We never met up again, but we did talk a little and even now there is the odd comment or like of a photo on Facebook.

The drive home actually had more impact on what came next rather than the bedroom activities of the previous evening. Around about halfway home I received a call on my mobile from my brother-in-law. Tony had purchased some new alloy wheels for his son for Christmas and was on his way over to my house to hide them in my garage.

Now this was not a strange call at all, and I could easily have just said, 'I am out at the minute, be home in about an hour if that's okay?' but I was flustered and I was paranoid that whatever I said, I was about to out myself. I mentioned Southampton and that just lead to more questions. I was staying with a friend last night, I added, another question was asked. Why would I elaborate further, I was single, I was always at home, Tony knew that so why would I mention a friend in Southampton?

Tony wasn't suspicious at all, it was all in my head, but it made my mind up that before I pursued any further relationships I was going to come out to my family. My sister Beverley, Tony's wife, found out at a drunken party night at my house, not totally the plan but it did the job. Angela, my oldest sister followed but I don't exactly recall a conversation, and I also came out to a friend from work, Hugo, who I had stayed with after my divorce while waiting for the purchase of my new house to go through.

Sometime following that, on a Friday afternoon I believe, I announced to Hugo at work my intention to stop at my parents' house on the way home and tell them. He asked if I was sure, and I was. I do not know why I picked that day, but something just made me do it. On the way to their house, I phoned Bev from the car and told her what I was about to do. Oh Lord! She wanted me to call her back as soon as I had done it.

I arrived unannounced not long after 5pm in the middle of my parents eating their tea, which they would not have expected (and yes, your evening meal is called tea and not dinner for any doubters). They offered me a drink and then we all sat in the lounge. We made small talk before I announced I had something to tell them, and they may not like it very much. My mum asked if I was getting back with Jill, and I jokingly reassured them it wasn't as bad as that. Then I just told them. I'm gay.

My mum spoke first and said something along the lines of, 'We made a lot of mistakes with your sister, and I am not going to make them again, so whatever makes you happy is okay'. This referred to my older sister Angela, who had come out when she was a teenager, in the early eighties, when times were very different. She did not receive the support she deserved, to say the least.

My father commented that I looked really worried, to which I said I was a bit worried about what Hayley and Aaron might say. He reassured me it would be fine; it was no big deal these days. I was a little dumbfounded. This was not the reaction I had expected. When I had been speaking to Hugo, he had asked what if they don't accept it, and I had contemplated briefly and concluded they probably wouldn't, but I really didn't care, I was ready to move on. Now, in reality I am sure rejection would have floored me, if not right then, in time, so I am very pleased it went that well, although my father would withdraw slightly later down the line, but that is another story we will get to.

On my way back home, I called my sisters to tell them how it had gone, and both were as surprised as I had been. Bev was now anticipating the call from my mother to discuss it further and Ang, on hearing my mums opening statement, called me a bastard for getting it so easy. I think she meant it affectionately.

One of the most important people I had to tell was my ex-wife Jill, and I was more worried about telling her than anyone else. Again, I got inside my own head and was worried if she took it badly, she could turn the kids against me. I hatched a plan to try and minimise the damage.

Aaron had now started secondary school and was due to go away on a school trip for a week, to Germany I think but I don't wholly remember, there was a lot going on in my head around that time. We would both be at the school early on the morning of the trip to wave off the coach, so I asked Jill if she could hang around after the coach left as I needed a chat. My theory was, if she exploded over the issue, Aaron would be out of the country for a week and Jill would have time to calm down before she said anything to him that might be damaging.

There was absolutely no reason for me to worry, Jill was a great comfort on that day and gave me the biggest hug and reassured me she would be there to support me when I was ready to tell the kids. I think from the look on my face she was concerned I was going to tell her I was dying so being gay was somewhat of a relief.

I decided to take a little more time before telling Hayley and Aaron, there seemed no rush until a potential relationship came along, although that didn't take as long as I thought. In the meantime, I continued to chat to a few people online and there were a couple of significant friendships made, the most notable being James. He was from Liverpool, and he spoke to dead people.

I should clarify. James was an enigma and interested me deeply from when I first chatted to him online. Without doubt I had a crush on him, and we would chat into the early hours about everything under the sun. We didn't really have too much in common and his spirituality was probably one of our most polar differences, but it very much intrigued me. I had never met anyone who had a spirit guide and worked as a medium.

Eventually our conversations got to the inevitable point where one of us suggested meeting, I suggested meeting on this occasion, and before long I was happily on the road to Liverpool for the night. I arrived before noon, on a Saturday morning, and we had a great afternoon lunching and walking around the Tate on the redeveloped Royal Albert Docks.

It hadn't been discussed but I wasn't going to be driving back home from Liverpool on the same day, so I checked into a hotel, and we spent the evening having drinks in the hotel bar. At some point we decided to take drinks up to the room and continue our conversation there. I remember we kissed in the lift and this night ended, as you might expect, in bed, but there is no need to elaborate on that.

We genuinely did go up to the room to continue our conversation, albeit this somehow ended up being in our underwear, and we did drink and chat for hours before the hormones took over. The spirituality was what interested me most and I half-jokingly asked James to tell me something about myself. He pondered then announced the name 'Stephen' had some significant meaning to me. It did not, but as you may expect, I will come back to this later.

I still know James, he has been down to visit a couple of times over the years, and we have fallen out of touch for periods, but now and again we touch base with a brief hello. Could we have had a relationship? I don't think so, but I still care for him, and I hope he feels the same way.

Before we move on, I feel this may be the appropriate point for a whistle-stop recap on a few relevant parts from my younger years. My attraction to men did not miraculously develop when I hit my thirties, it has always been there but I have so far edited it from my history so I could spring the big reveal. Let's go back and fill in a few gaps.

I would say my first awareness was of a completely non-sexual nature and relates to my friendship with Eugene in Germany. I was a pretty innocent child regards sex. I had once seen quite an explicit pornographic magazine one of the older boys had when first arriving in Germany, aged only nine, but it wasn't stirring me. Not really surprising at that age.

Although completely platonic, the friendship with Eugene was powerful, coming at the cusp of puberty for me, and when he left, I was truly heartbroken. I think that was my first experience of loving someone.

When puberty did explode, just before leaving Germany, I have already mentioned the explorations I engaged in with Helen, and I briefly referred to a boy with whom I engaged in a little show me yours and I'll show you mine. The episodes with the boy, a neighbour I remember but will leave unnamed, were much more hands on than I described, more frequent and more enjoyable.

The return to England, and having to get to know a whole new friendship group, lead to a hiatus in all but self-exploration. After a few years, there was a sleepover incident with a school friend in which we both masturbated to some of his father's porn. Initially he was in the bathroom, and I was in his bedroom, but he apparently finished first and walked in on me. He stood and watched, and I didn't stop.

Around this time was also the trip to Kilvrough. I claimed my bravado in leading the march to the showers was all confidence related, and to a degree it was, but equal motivation was the voyeuristic reward of seeing all my friends naked.

I talked to girls at school too, and I remember trying to woo one in particular with a Valentine's gift, but she only wanted to be friends. I did also briefly go out with a girl called Maxime but that was a deliberate act to allow me to spend more time with Darren. Darren was absolutely my first ever crush. I actually dreamt about him on more than one occasion, and would also find myself thinking about him during my frequent moments of private contemplation.

I have talked about becoming more interested in fashion during this period too, and my parents allowing me to choose my own clothes with my allowance. The main obsession I omitted was an interest in underwear which has remained until this day. Back then I had discovered the tanga brief, a triangle of material front and back held together with elastic side straps. I loved them. Nowadays I am a brief man, Tommy Hilfiger being a particular favourite, and if you have any interest whatsoever you can find me on Instagram, more often than not, displaying them to my 25,000+ followers. I know! Who'd have thought a middle-aged man in pants would be so popular.

The next move was to Bampton and my reading list expanded from the horrors of Stephen King and James Herbert to the gay coming of age stories of Edmund White. I had been browsing books in the local bookshop and a cover caught my eye. It was *A Boy's Own Story*, and the cover was of a young man wearing a vest top, nothing particularly revealing but I picked it up. On reading the blurb on the back I was immediately interested and decided to make a purchase, probably sweating irrationally at the till in fear that the assistant knew the theme of every book in the shop and was judging me.

While living in Bampton I referenced travelling with my friends to London on shopping trips to Oxford Street and Carnaby Street. I failed to mention on one of the trips I purchased a fingerless leather glove to accompany the cross-on-a-hoop earring I was wearing to complete my George Michael, *Faith* look. On another trip I managed to find a copy of another musical favourite's autobiography, Barry Manilow's *Sweet Heaven*. What can I say, the signs were there I'm telling you!

The next thing that happened was profound in my life, upsets me still, and relates to when my friendship with Ian ended. When hinting at it earlier in the book I referred to it as a sliding doors moment and I truly think it was. I said I wasn't naming the people who have done me wrong, and I considered omitting Ian's name but when I reflect, he didn't do anything wrong at all, it was just a different time.

Ian was my second crush but this time I was older, and I was ready to tell him how I felt because I wanted him badly and the feeling was only growing. The trigger came when he announced he was moving away from Bampton, and I had a gut-wrenching feeling I would lose contact as I had with Darren. He only moved to the next town, but I already saw him much less so one day I wrote him a letter, a love letter by all accounts.

I think it is fair to say my feelings were not reciprocated and Ian has not spoken to me since. I tried to explain, I tried to backtrack, but the letter was pretty clear about how I felt so it was hard to undo the damage at that point. If this situation had played out differently, if Ian had felt the same, I can only imagine what different direction my life would have taken.

Although I wish Ian had stood by me, if only as a friend if uninterested, the credit I do give to him and the reason I use his name is, to my knowledge, he never told my secret to anyone else. None of our mutual friends ever mentioned anything, no diatribe of gay hatred emerged and other than my broken heart, life went on as normal, minus Ian.

It would be simple to claim this incident scared me back into the closet, but I really didn't feel like that at the time. I have discussed this with my elder sister at length, she is bemused that I did not know I was gay, especially with having an elder sister who had already come out. She assumed I must have been living in misery all those years, but I really wasn't.

I believe my sexuality was truly naive, or maybe just ahead of its time. If I liked a girl, I liked a girl, if I liked a boy, I liked a boy. That seems to be the norm these days, doesn't it? The other question you get in this situation is, 'Are you bisexual then?'. I guess if you had asked me back then in the middle of it all then maybe I would have agreed but following my divorce and finally fully exploring my sexuality I know now I am truly a gay man, and always have been.

Just to finish, after Ian I spent the three years or so with Sian. After Sian there were a mixture of girls and guys, ranging from kisses to condoms, and then I met Jill and we are pretty much back to where I left off in my biographical tale.

Maybe now it makes more sense why there was a thread of male nudity and a gay outing theme running through my St Philip's story.

CHAPTER 13

Coles pulled slowly up the drive to his house and parked the car in front of the garage. The weather looked like more snow, but he could not be bothered to put the car in the garage, maybe later.

The double glazing on the house made it difficult to hear cars pulling up outside, and although Coles wasn't intentionally quiet when entering the house, Martin obviously never heard him.

Coles walked across to the living room, but when he reached the door, he didn't go in. Instead, he looked through the opening and could see Martin sitting in the front of the television. When Coles looked more closely, he could see that Martin was watching a scene from the rental movie he had hired the night before. The film had an adult rating, and the particular scene Martin was watching was quite sexually explicit. Coles watched as Martin paused the picture, watched in slow motion, then rewound the scene and watched it again.

Coles went back to the front door and was deliberately noisy so that Martin would hear him. He went into the kitchen to give his son time to rewind the film and put it back in its box. He had no intention of mentioning the incident, after all these things had to be learnt, although Coles made himself a mental note to have that father to son talk before too long.

After a few minutes Martin came into the kitchen and from the overly innocent look on his face, Coles was sure he would have suspected something even if he had not already known.

'You're home early,' Martin said.

'Yeah! Thought we could get a video. I've got one to take back anyway,' Coles replied.

'Oh! Have you?' Martin said, trying to sound surprised. 'I'll come with you then and see what they've got.'

They had tea, and Martin washed the dishes while Coles took a shower. They walked to the shops. It didn't take very long to choose a film, and they were back in the house within an hour of leaving. As they went back in Coles looked once more at the car, then the garage. He could still not be bothered.

They enjoyed the video, although they would both rather have been watching John's previous choice, and when it was over Martin was ready for bed.

'Have you brushed your teeth?'

'Yes!'

'Okay. I'll be up in a minute to tuck you in.'

'DAD!'

'Dad nothing, you're never too old to be tucked in, besides, I want to have a talk.'

Martin was instantly worried that his father knew about him watching the other video. He quickly made his way upstairs praying that his father would decide not to bother with the talk.

Coles rewound the film and tidied around the room. He had a cup of coffee then went upstairs for an early night. He washed and changed into his dressing gown, then went in to see Martin.

'Are you still awake?' he spoke softly.

For a moment Martin considered pretending then decided not to bother.

'Yes,' he replied, as he sat up and turned on the bedside lamp.

'I've been thinking. How would you like to go to boarding school?' Coles asked, not knowing how Martin would react.

'What, St Philip's?'

'Doesn't have to be, you don't have to go at all if you don't want to, but I just wondered if you had ever thought about it.'

'Didn't ever cross my mind before,' Martin said, as he considered the idea.

'Well why don't you think about it. You do have to spend a lot of time on your own, and if you were at boarding school you could be with friends instead of with me all the time.'

'What about when I come home? Would you be here, or would you be working?'

'We could arrange it so I'm here of course,' Coles said. 'It's just if you did want to, now would be a good time. You've only just started secondary school, so you won't have missed much.'

'Do you want me to go?'

'I'd like you to get a good education, but I'm not going to force you into it, and I know it would be hard at first, not being able to see each other, but it might be worth it.'

'I don't know. People say things about private schools, and I don't want all my friends calling me names. But it might be good fun.'

Coles could see Martin was considering the idea and began to wonder how he would feel if he did decide to go. When Coles had been a boy he had always wanted to go to boarding school, but his father had not been able to afford it. Coles did not have his father's problem but was unsure how he would feel not being able to see Martin for weeks at a time. He had fought so hard to keep him when he was a baby, and now he was asking him if he wanted to leave. Then there was the murder, not the greatest of examples.

'Tell you what, why don't you think about it for a while, then we can talk about it again,' Coles said. 'In the meantime, how do you fancy going to the Christmas concert at St Philip's?'

'Sure!' came the reply. Martin would not normally have been so enthusiastic, but St Philip's was the talk of his schoolyard, and any chance he had to go there was a chance to make a few of his friends jealous.

'Okay. Goodnight then,' Coles said as he left the room. He would normally have kissed his son goodnight but this time he resisted. He knew Martin did not really like it anymore.

Martin, who had been expecting the usual kiss, turned off his light and lay down. For a moment he wondered why his father had not kissed him, then he thought he understood. That night he slept well, and all the friction of the last few days filed itself away in his memory as he dreamt.

Next morning Martin and John were up together. Coles wrote Martin a note to explain his absence from school while Martin read the cartoons in the paper. When Coles had finished the letter, they swapped.

'Damn!' Coles exclaimed as he read the headline.

'What?' Martin asked, but he had seen the paper and knew exactly what it was his father was referring to. 'So, it's true what they say about private schools' Martin thought to himself.

The headline read:

GAY HEADMASTER MURDER SUSPECT

It was just what Coles had not wanted. He read the story briefly, finished his breakfast, then made a move to leave.

'Don't forget to lock up when you go for the bus,' Coles reminded.

'I won't,' Martin replied, then leant over and kissed his father on the cheek. 'See you later.'

Coles smiled.

Outside the air was crisp and fresh snow lay on the ground, and on the car. Coles was still clearing the snow from his car when Martin left for the bus and was still there when his neighbour reversed his snow free car from his garage. Coles cursed himself for being so lazy the night before.

When he finally got going, he went straight to the station to pick up Bradey, then onto St Philip's. He had a few new ideas to check out and he felt sure he was close to discovering the truth.

Ankle-deep in snow, and considerably deeper in thought, Michael stood on the bank of a small stream that ran through a patch of trees on the perimeter of the school grounds. His eyes were glazed over as his mind concentrated on the past.

The first time he had been to this part of the grounds Jaymi, Carl, Andrew and Ben had been with him. It was early October, the previous year, and only Michael's third day at the school. The other boys had started the term in September, but Michael had been unable to begin with them due to being in Germany with his family. His father's posting there was coming to an end, and the family were spending the last few weeks together before Michael went away to school, and the rest of his family; parents, and younger sister, moved on to Cyprus.

The sky was clear, the wind bitter and the previous night's frost had only partially thawed. The last leaves of autumn fought in the breeze for freedom from their twig fingered captors, aided by the vigorous shaking of branches caused by the rope swing upon which Jaymi and Carl played.

Andrew tutted as he looked on. He warned against accidents as Ben ran and jumped on to the rope swing.

Michael also stood watching from the side, but not through choice. He would have loved to join in with the fun but being only three days old at the school he still felt awkward. Although the rest of the boys had only known each other a short while, Michael's late start had made a difference. The others played as though they had been lifelong friends and Michael still had to make that bond.

Just then Andrew's warnings proved valid. The branch over which the rope swing was hung snapped. Jaymi, Carl and Ben flew through the air and landed on the bank of the stream. Carl and Ben had somehow managed to recover through the fall and landed on their feet on the side of the ditch above which they swung, stumbling to the top with only muddied shoes. Jaymi was not so lucky and planted into the side of the bank with his knees before falling backwards, finishing sitting down in a squelch of mud and thawing leaves at the bottom of the ditch.

'Shit!' Jaymi cursed as he climbed back out. 'I've already got two uniform warnings, I'm gonna get detention when they see the state of this.

Michael saw an opportunity to endear himself to the group and kicked off his shoes with his heels, undid his belt, and removed his trousers. His growth spurt had only just started so he was only slightly taller than Jaymi at this stage so they should fit close enough. He stood in his blazer and pants, socks getting wet in the snow, and offered his trousers to Jaymi.

'Swap, they aren't going to give me a detention in my first week,' he said.

The boys swapped trousers and their friendship was bonded for the rest of their lives, or for the rest of Jaymi's life at least.

By the time Coles and Bradey arrived at the school it was snowing again. Coles had to fight to keep control of the car as he swerved to avoid a group of children playing on the drive. They ran off before Coles had a chance to shout after them, but it soon left his mind as he saw Michael walking slowly across the yard towards the church. He looked so sad. Coles felt for him.

'What's lined up for today then sir?' Bradey asked eagerly.

'Find out who wrote the letter, and if it wasn't Jaymi then I don't think Price is our man.'

'How can you be sure?' Bradey asked.

'Because Price used to teach Jaymi and read out some of his poems in class, so he would know Jaymi's handwriting. If Jaymi didn't write the letter, why would Price kill him?'

'Well why don't we just ask Michael?' Bradey asked. 'It seems like he wrote it. He would be able to confirm it if he had.'

'Well yes, I'm pretty certain Michael wrote it, but I'd rather not confront him with it just yet. He's going through enough just losing a friend let alone thinking his letter may have had something to do with it.'

Coles pulled up outside the main entrance.

'I thought we could take a look in their English classroom, there's bound to be a sample of some handwriting they've done in there.'

They both left the car and headed for the secretary's office. They would need directions to the correct English room.

As they waited, while Julie checked the files on the boys, Mr Price walked in with some empty boxes in his arms. He looked over at Coles in disgust, then passed silently into his office.

'The board of governors have told him to move his stuff out at the weekend,' Julie whispered. 'It's been all over the papers about him. I feel sorrier for his wife though.'

Coles and Bradey said nothing, and in a short time they had the information they needed and were on their way to the appropriate classroom.

When they reached their destination, they found the room empty. Classes had been abandoned for the rest of the week and the teachers were taking turns to patrol the playground. There was a shelf at the back of the class with several exercise books on it and Coles began by searching through the pile labelled '2W', which he was reliably informed was Jaymi's class.

He pulled out two of the books and placed the rest back on the shelf. He first looked through Jaymi's. It was obvious at first glance that it was not Jaymi's handwriting in the letter, but Coles read on. He laughed quietly as he read and when Bradey inquired as to why, he read again aloud:

> *Excuse me ma'am but could I have some toothpaste*
> *Yes, I know I bought three tubes just yesterday*
> *What I'd really like to buy would be a tonic*
> *To make this nervous feeling go away*
>
>
> *I'll try a chemist further down the high street*
> *Perhaps there'll be a man to serve me there*
> *But when I walked in, I saw my best friends' mother*
> *I bought a can of something for my hair*
>
> *I've tried all sources in the local area*
> *There's really only one thing left for me*
> *I'll pay a visit to the 'George & Dragon'*
> *And buy some quite discreetly when I pee*

'Quite the little funny man wasn't he,' Bradey remarked.

'Yes, but not the letter writer.'

Coles felt relieved. He feared his handwriting theory was too weak, but the differences in style were too obvious for an informed person to mistake. Jaymi's book was returned to the pile and Michael's was checked for a match. It did. Bradey seconded.

'Now I'm certain Price is the wrong man. If there was no letter maybe, but the letter in the fire suggests that Price read it, thought it was from Jaymi so killed him to cover his tracks. But there's no way Price would have mistaken Michael's writing for Jaymi's.'

'So, the letter must have been planted in the fire by the real killer, who did mistake the writing, to try and frame Price when they heard he was being questioned.' Bradey looked at Coles for confirmation.

'Yes, but who would have found McWinney's drug dealing reason enough to kill him, and a witness?'

'And have little knowledge of the boy's hand-writing,' Bradey added.

Coles thought for a moment then his face lit up as it struck him.

'Of course!' he said, then left the English class in a hurry to pursue his train of thought.

'Who?' Bradey begged as he ran after him.

ANALYSIS 13

I am starting to think I may have been somewhat preoccupied with sex at the age I was writing my St Philip's story. Maybe not surprising for a teenager trying to navigate his sexuality, losing his virginity, and experimenting with both genders but I am sure even those not going through this same process have paused a movie on a nude scene, haven't they?

I don't mean now, I don't mean online, I don't mean on SKY, I mean on an old VHS video recorder. Those blasted fuzzy lines always crossing the screen over exactly the part you wanted to see in more detail, not that the resolution when paused was good enough to see anything anyway. We must have had much better imaginations back then.

The boarding school conversation never happened in my own life, but I often wondered if I would have preferred it to moving around all the time. I can only imagine how it may have worked out, but my parents were not the type to send their kids away for education, taking quite some persuading just to allow my sister to remain in Germany for a few months to finish her exams.

The poem is mine. After I left school and got my first job in the warehouse in Witney, one of the women working alongside me was a poet and speech writer. I think she was working there temporarily for some extra money to support her son as she was either going through or was recently divorced. I had shared my writing aspirations with her, and I also attempted a few funny poems in her style, her style being very much Pam Ayres style in fact.

There are only another two chapters left to tidy up this whole mystery and Coles is on to a new train of thought, stitching the clues together. Have you worked it out yet? All the pieces are there I think, there isn't going to be some dubious twist you could never have foreseen. I'm pretty happy with the thread of clues and distractions, although I am conscious nobody else has read it yet. Now I am getting nearer to the end, I am beginning to feel a bit nervous about sharing the whole thing.

Before I carry on with my coming-out escapades, I have a small confession to make regard the last chapter. I said from the start that I would leave the original story untouched to provide some insight into my writing capability at the time but, when reading back through chapter thirteen, I came across a comment in bold reminding me to come back and finish a section of text.

I had no idea until now I hadn't completed the story and I am not sure why I left this gap to come back to later. I remembered exactly what was supposed to be there all these years later and contemplated leaving it unfinished, as it is not a piece that has any real bearing on the outcome. Instead, I decided to complete it, doing my best to keep faithful to my original intention. I have inserted 199 words and I think they blend with the original reasonably well, but maybe you can spot them.

I am quite enjoying weaving my biography through the chapters of the fiction, finding it quite therapeutic in fact, and without any real pre-planning it is apt that the gay headmaster headline has fallen slap bang in the middle of my own coming out story. The only important people left to tell were my children, Hayley and Aaron, and the series of events leading to this were initiated by James, in a roundabout way, so I will carry on from there.

Unlike the trip to Southampton, when I returned from Liverpool, James and myself continued to talk regularly and a little while later, we decided a return visit from him down to me would be a good idea. James got the train to Birmingham, and I picked him up from the station and drove us back down to where I was living in Carterton, and we had another great weekend catching up.

On the Saturday night we were going out into Oxford and through the course of our chatting it transpired I had no idea about the gay bars or clubs in Oxford as I had never been. We ordered a taxi and as soon as we hopped in James asked the driver if he knew where the gay bars were in Oxford, he did, and we were off. I wasn't used to being so open, but I liked it.

We were dropped off on Paradise Street and I experienced my first ever visit to a gay bar at The Castle Tavern, followed by a night dancing in Cloud 9, a nightclub above the old Westgate shopping centre. Cloud 9 is long gone, and

The Castle no longer flies the rainbow flag, but I have great memories of both places from this night and many other nights to follow.

James went back on the Sunday, or maybe even the Monday, from Oxford station this time and we hugged before he left. A public display of affection with a man which again was my first time. We kept in touch, exchanged Christmas presents even, but there was never any real question between us about starting a long-distance relationship, however, I really was beginning to feel like I wanted something more than one-night stands and internet friends.

The point I was trying to get to with the story of James' visit is that he had introduced me to the Oxford gay scene, and I had enjoyed it. Enjoyed it so much that the very next weekend I went back on my own to The Castle Tavern and, buoyed with confidence from the previous weekend, I even chatted someone up that I had taken a liking too.

David had gone there to meet someone else but luckily for me they were a no-show. Cloud 9 happened again, and Dave came back to mine that night, which I accept sounds like the type of one-night stand I just said I wasn't looking for, however, we ended up together for five years, so I forgive myself. Of course, the prospect of a serious relationship meant it was time to tell my children.

I spoke to Jill and let her know that I planned to tell them, and then proceeded to work myself up into a bit of a frenzy of nerves before each conversation but all in all it was a bit of a non-event to be honest. Hayley, being that much older, was fine. Surprised of course but she has only ever supported me. Hayley will be thirty-five this year and I have been her father for all but four years of it, and she has been my daughter.

Aaron was only twelve and I had concerns he may get bullied once this news was out, but his response was equally as accepting as his sister. He was staying over at my house the weekend I told him and was a little quiet at first, not really knowing what to say. He went up to his room to do something and I quickly messaged Jill to say the deed was done and he seemed okay. Jill had kept her weekend clear and offered to come and pick him up if it all went wrong.

Not only did it not go wrong but not too long afterwards I was tearfully delighted to find out that Aaron had actually told his friends. He took it all in his stride, he didn't seem to care if people at school knew, and none of his friends ever had an issue with it to my knowledge. He would still have friends sleep over at mine, and when he was an older teenager, he would bring a friend or two over if we were having a house party, which happened quite often, I was the cool gay dad now.

I am going to skip quickly through my relationship with David, not because it wasn't important, it very much was, but because something even bigger happened during that time which I am going to focus on.

David was my first serious gay relationship, and we would have some great times together, fantastic holidays and make good friends that I still see regularly now. We lived together, got a dog, and got engaged before our relationship came to an end, not for any dramatic reason, but simply because we were drifting apart.

David was retraining as a nurse and was attending Oxford Brookes university as part of his studies. He was spending a lot of time there and with a new set of friends he had made, and it just wasn't working out anymore. This is the second time a nursing career has fucked up my relationship, and to think I have recently been clapping for the frickin' NHS! I jest, of course.

The final straw came when David announced he didn't think he was going to be able to come on the summer holiday we had booked with friends because of his studies, even though it was still over six months away and I would be celebrating my fortieth birthday while we were there. I suggested we should maybe call it a day and we did.

Much sadder than David leaving was having to rehome our dog, Jake. I had tried to keep him after Dave left but I had to commute for work and was spending long days away from home. Even with a dog walker it just wasn't fair on him. David couldn't take him, as he was now in student accommodation, so I took the tough decision to let him go.

He was such a beautiful black & white Springer Spaniel and he seemed very happy when he hopped in the back of the people carrier with the chosen family when they came back to pick him up. I hope he had a great time growing older with the two young boys who seemed so excited to have him. He would be fourteen now, so he could still be out there somewhere pottering around, I guess.

I will just tell one funny story which happened after we had separated. It must have been six months, or more likely even eighteen months, after we had split as I was at a summer barbecue, and I had separated from David not long after Christmas. The friends we were dining with had also been friends of Dave and I think we were all aware he was now dating a porn star. My phone rings and David is calling me, which is odd as we haven't really kept in touch other than a Facebook like or similar.

I can tell from David's voice that he is a bit stressed and upset and I manage to calm him a little and get him to explain what is going on. It transpires he is calling me from London where he is having an engagement party with his boyfriend, and he has just told the group he is with that he was going to the toilet, but he has in fact left the building and doesn't want to go back as he doesn't want to get engaged to the guy after all.

Not sure how I can help from seventy miles away, I manage to establish that another mutual friend, John, is at the party in Soho, and Dave has trotted off to Oxford Street. I tell Dave to wait where he is and then I phone John and break the news Dave has done a runner. We cannot help but find it amusing but John heads off to find Dave and I left it for the two of them to sort out. Needless to say, the wedding was off.

Dave is now married to someone else, another Richard in fact, and they have adopted two little boys. We don't keep in touch anymore, nothing really happened but one day I received the fatal unfriending on social media. I like that he called me when he needed help though, I never stop caring about the people I have known, I like that about myself.

The story I want to focus on from that period came about as a result of David moving in with me. Prior to living together, my parents used to visit me almost every Saturday for a coffee on their way home from shopping. Despite being very accepting when I had come out to them, when Dave moved in these visits stopped completely.

I wasn't too disturbed by it, I would still get phone calls and they would ask how we both were, I just put it down to probably my father not liking any awkwardness. Ironically, my father's actions were about to cause a lot more awkwardness than not visiting me could ever have avoided. I will tell you my experience of the story first and then I will tell you the events leading up to it, as relayed to me by my sister as I was not present for main drama.

We had just returned from a weekend away and almost before we had put our bags down the house phone was ringing. I answered and it was my mother, sounding obviously distressed. I asked if everything was okay and did she want me to come over, genuinely concerned I was about to hear some awful news, but she said it was okay and she could just tell me over the phone. What she told me was, before my parents were together, at the age of seventeen, my mother had given birth to a baby boy, and he had been adopted. I had an older brother.

I'm a bit blurry on the rest of the conversation other than to say I reassured her not to worry, it was a long time ago, in Ireland, and people's choices were not their own. I asked if he had been in touch and if that was why she was telling me, but he hadn't, there has never been any contact, but she wanted me to know. Genuinely feeling dazed, the dizzy headed feeling you get when you have a bad fever, I put down the phone and announced to Dave I had a brother.

My sister Beverley is the hub of our family and I called her once I had taken a breath, I knew she would know more. The previous day my parents had been at my sister's house for lunch, I am thinking it may even have been Easter weekend. Drinks were flowing, as always when our family gets together, and something must have sparked a conversation about the fact they were no longer visiting me at weekends.

During the course of the conversation my mother, no doubt fuelled with gin, took a stance against my father, announcing, 'I have lost one son, I am not losing another one!'

As you can imagine, eyebrows were raised, and my sister questioned for more details, at first thinking maybe a miscarriage or cot death, only to be told an equally harrowing story surrounding the adoption.

My mother is still alive, and this is not a subject we talk about. I am also conscious it will be upsetting should she read about it, but I feel it is part of the story I need to tell. I will keep it brief for my mother's sake.

The pregnancy followed a girl's holiday which must have happened around a month before my mother's seventeenth birthday. I can only imagine how the news was received by the family, but they stopped short of sending her away to the workhouse and it was discussed that one of the older sisters could take the child on as her own, presumably with the pregnancy being concealed in some way.

The older sister had two boys of her own and this offer only seemed to stand should my mother give birth to a girl, so on the birth of a son the offer was rescinded, and he was to be adopted. I am not sure if this last-minute change of heart or some other event complicated matters but for some reason the adoption was not enacted efficiently with the child's removal at the hospital, and my mother took her son home and cared for him for almost three months before then being separated from him.

The final tragedy of the whole event is that, not long afterwards my mother and father would get together, having known each other from childhood. My father knew what had happened and they tried to get my brother back, but it was too late, it could not be undone, and to this day there has been no contact.

I have chased down a copy of his birth certificate, but I stopped short of registering with the relevant agencies. I have considered writing to *Long Lost Families*, the ancestry tracking TV show, with the story but I am sure they would have wanted me to have conducted my own enquiries first.

Yesterday I also received a call from my father to say a family friend had passed away, Tanya Moncur, someone I knew when I was younger, only a year or two older than me. Maybe I would prefer not to know what happened in case it is not a happy ending, but I suspect curiosity will get the better of me at some point.

To try and finish on a slightly more uplifting note, following these revelations my parents would start to visit again at the weekends for a coffee with me and Dave.

Oh, and one more thing to add to the growing list of life's mysteries, my brother's name at birth was Stephen. The name I had been told was very important in my life by my psychic friend James on my visit to Liverpool. I appreciate Stephen is not an uncommon name so this could all very easily be coincidence, and I would still very much consider myself a sceptic, but there is something about that James. Something that makes me question my own beliefs.

CHAPTER 14

For once Coles knew where in the school he was going. He walked briskly across the yard towards the field on the left side of the main drive. On the way into the school, he had noticed Mr Davies had been there, and as they now approached, they could see he still was.

Davies, who had noticed them coming, stopped what he was doing and sent away the boy who was helping him.

'Looks serious,' Davies said as Coles and Bradey stopped before him.

'No,' Coles lied. 'Just a couple of questions.'

'Fire away.'

'You have quite a strong involvement with the anti-drugs in sport association I believe?' Coles started.

'Yes.'

'No doubt you've read the papers and know about McWinney selling drugs to the pupils?'

'Yes.'

'Did you know before you read the paper?'

'No, I didn't know, and I didn't kill him if that's where this is leading.'

'Where were you when he fell?'

'I was in the sports hall sorting out some of the equipment. I had a free period.'

'Were you with anyone?' Bradey added to the questioning.

'No, I was suspiciously alone,' Davies joked.

'Do you take any other classes except for games?' Coles changed tact.

'No, I'm purely physical.'

Coles was silent for a moment while he searched his jacket pockets for Michael's letter. He found it and showed it to Davies, alert for any reaction it may cause.

'Have you seen this before?'

Davies scanned the letter then looked up at Coles.

'Sorry, it's no again.'

'What about the handwriting? Do you know who's it is?' Coles couldn't help but smile as he asked the question.

'Yes, funnily enough, is it Michael Bracher's?'

The smile was gone from Coles' face in an instant. The answer was supposed to be 'Jaymi' or at least 'no'.

'You said you didn't teach the boys, so how can you be sure?'

'Well,' Davies explained. 'If it had been anybody else, I wouldn't have known. You see, Michael broke his arm last holiday and he's not been able to do games. When the others were doing sports, I sometimes asked him to write some stories to keep him busy. I couldn't be certain, but it is very similar.'

'Thank you,' Coles said before walking away.

'Where were you when Jaymi had his accident?' Bradey asked, not so keen to give up on Davies.

'I was taking his class for rugby. I sent him back to get changed because he didn't feel too good. I did leave the class though. Mr Price came to tell me there was a phone call. I went to take it and, on my way back, the fire bell rang so I went outside with everybody else.'

Bradey also thanked Davies, then turned and caught up with Coles.

'He doesn't have an alibi for either murder,' Bradey said as he came alongside Coles.

'No, but he knew it was Michael's writing in the letter.'

'What if Jaymi was killed for some other reason and not because of the letter.'

'I was thinking that myself,' Coles said. 'Which would mean Michael is still in danger if Davies or Price are the killer.'

'Why don't we go and see Michael, maybe he can tell us something new.'

Coles agreed and they both walked off towards the church. As they crossed the drive Bradey noticed a snowball heading his way. He ducked and promptly fell over in the snow. Coles chose to ignore him and walked on. He waited for Bradey at the back of the church and greeted him with a witty comment before they walked down the aisle to where Michael sat.

The boys were performing their final dress rehearsal before tomorrow's concert and Michael was staring at the front row of the choir where Jaymi should have been. The choir master had thought it touching to leave his space unoccupied, and the boy to the right of Jaymi's place now sang the solos.

Michael and Coles exchanged greetings and for a moment sat and listened to the music.

'I just wanted to ask you a couple of questions,' Coles said quietly.

Mr Sheppard spun on his heels and gave Coles a deadly glare. He obviously had not been quiet enough.

Michael stood up and motioned Coles and Bradey towards the exit.

'We can talk outside,' he said in a much calmer voice than when they had first spoken.

They left the church and stood in silence outside until a passing boy was out of earshot before continuing their conversation.

'Can you think of any reason why someone would want to kill Jaymi?' Coles asked. He didn't want to upset Michael, but he really did need some answers.

'Only what I told you before. Mr Price must have thought it was Jaymi that saw him upstairs, and not me.'

'Well, we don't think Mr Price was responsible. We found this letter in his room.' Coles took the letter from his pocket as he spoke and handed it to Michael. 'If he had read this then he would have known it was you. You did write it I presume?'

'Yes, I wrote it, but I already posted it.' Michael was confused as to how it had come to be in Price's room.

'It seems it was never sent, and we believe Jaymi may have been killed because McWinney's murderer thought Jaymi had written it,' Bradey tactlessly explained.

'You mean he was killed because of my letter?' Michael's voice faltered and his eyes, already bloodshot from hours of sobbing, began to well with tears once more.

Coles glared at Bradey with the same contempt the choir master had shown when Coles had spoken over the choir in church. Bradey realised his thoughtlessness at once.

'You didn't sign the letter, did you?' Coles asked.

'No, I never do when I write to a friend.' Michael was silent for a few moments then added, 'Jaymi posted it.' There was an awful realisation in his voice. 'It was the day you came to our dorm. He had to go to a detention, and I asked him to post it on his way. Remember?'

'Where would it have been posted?' Coles asked. He remembered the incident and was encouraged by it.

'Each floor has its own post box. One of the seniors empties it and takes them to the office. The post van collects from the office each night.'

'Right! I think we better have a word with the lad who emptied it. I don't suppose you know who it was?'

'No, but there'll be a rota in the office.'

Coles thanked Michael for his help then he and Bradey left, after giving Michael instructions to wait in the church until an officer came over to look after him. Just to be safe.

They walked once more across the schoolyard to the main entrance and then on to Price's office. Julie was not at her desk when they arrived, so they entered Price's office unannounced.

Price was packing some books into a cardboard box. He had noticed them enter but carried on without looking up.

'I'm sorry about the papers,' Coles apologised.

'Well, that's all right then,' Price snapped back sarcastically.

'I am sorry. There was nothing I could do about it.' Coles almost did sound sorry too.

'Too late, the board of governors have decided it would be best for me to resign.'

'Well, before you go you could help me with something.'

'Help you! Why the hell should I do anything for you?'

'Look, don't push it. You're still a suspect,' Coles reminded him.

'I'd like to see some evidence.'

'Well, if you would be a bit more cooperative instead of wasting our time with your lies and self-pity, we might be able to prove you didn't do it.'

Coles was losing his patience with Price. Bradey, noticing this, stepped in on the conversation.

'What we would like is a copy of the mail collection rota.'

'Julie will give you a copy.'

'She's not there,' Bradey replied.

'Well then her twin sister will give you a copy.'

Price looked past both Bradey and the open door at Julie's desk. Bradey turned to see Julie was indeed back at her desk. Price went back to his packing and Coles and Bradey left the room to speak with Julie. They obtained a copy of the rota but before leaving Coles stepped back into Price's office.

'You won't be leaving just yet, will you?'

'No! I'm here until Sunday as headmaster and I don't have to vacate my house for three months, so you'll have no trouble getting hold of me. Is that all?'

'For now,' Coles said as he left.

Julie's directions lead them directly to the sixth form block. As they walked in all heads turned towards them. Coles went to the nearest boy and spoke softly so the others in the room could not hear.

'I'm looking for Jason Miller.'

The boy pointed to a door at the back of the room. Coles walked to it, knocked, then entered.

'Jason Miller?' he enquired of the three boys in the room.

'That's me,' the tallest of the three replied.

Coles moved towards Jason, and Bradey asked the other two boys to leave. He closed the door behind them, then removed his notepad and joined Coles.

'Right Jason, I'd like to ask you a few questions about your post collecting. Anything you'd like to say before I start?'

'How did you find out?' Jason asked, looking down at his feet.

Coles had yet to find anything out, but he played along.

'A little bird told me. Carry on.'

'Well, we had the idea a few months ago. One of the boys was emptying the post box and he noticed one of the envelopes was open. When he looked it had a birthday card with some money inside. Since then, we've been opening the ones that feel like cards, and if there's money in them, we take it out.'

'Haven't any of the boys noticed when their friends write back without a thank you?' Bradey asked.

'No, see what we do is swap the money for less. Say a ten-pound note for a fiver, then the intended still receives something to write back and thank for,' Jason explained as if it was a redeeming feature of the practice.

Things were beginning to fall into place.

'Is that what you did on the day Mr McWinney died?'

'Not me. That was Wednesday. I was doing some charity work at the local care centre Christmas party.' Jason blushed with embarrassment at the irony.

Coles' eyes wandered to meet Bradey's. Another twist, their eyes agreed.

'Who would have collected the mail in your absence?'

'Don't know, but the ones in on the scheme usually volunteer for as many extra days as they can.'

The three of them went back through to the main room. Coles had no need to attract the room's attention as all eyes were already turned in their direction.

'Does anyone remember who collected the mail on the day Mr McWinney died?'

There was a silence, then a voice spoke up from the back of the room.

'I think David Walton did, but he's not here. He left just after you came in.'

Coles and Bradey left the block with Jason in tow for identification purposes. It took only a few seconds to find him.

As they came out into the main yard, they noticed a crowd of boys looking over towards them. No, they were looking above them. Coles, Bradey and Jason looked up to see the cause of the crowds staring.

On the top floor, on a window ledge just along from the one McWinney had fallen from, sat a boy.

'That's David!' Jason said.

ANALYSIS 14

I appreciate self-praise is no recommendation, but I am really enjoying reading this story back and remembering how I weaved the plot together. I like that Mr Davies has been a suspicious character throughout, offering the reader an alternate to Mr Price should they have felt he was too obvious a suspect.

It's no *Line of Duty* I accept, of which I am currently watching the sixth series and we are still chasing the elusive 'H'. In my defence, I was a naive seventeen-year-old when I conceived my story and not even in *Line of Duty* is every clue completely subtle regardless of the overall quality of the end product. That little shit-head Ryan Pilkington on his bike dropping off burner phones in series one, now being a trainee constable though! Pure genius, the whole story linked back full circle to events in the past, what a good idea.

Carrying on, no sooner had Coles' suspicions lead him back to Mr Davies, this line of enquiry is closed with the realisation he recognised Michael's handwriting. Mr Price has almost certainly been ruled out for similar reasons, even though it was he who lured Mr Davies from the playing field leaving them both with no alibi for either murder. Do we even have another suspect?

Then the mic-drop moment arrives. It all links to the posting of the letter back in the same chapter as the broken tape-recorder. A critical chapter which lays down all the seeds for why a second murder took place, why there was a case of mistaken identity, as well as the clue for how the reader may have spotted the tape recorders presence as reason for suspicion, rather than an explanation for accidental death.

I clearly had given it a lot of thought and I really hope I was subtle enough for the final pieces to be present but undetected. Did you remember Jaymi posting the letter but being a little too late and having a confrontation with one of the sixth form students directly? Mr Price also present and snatching the letter from Jaymi, leaving himself as a suspect for any reader who picked up on it.

And when Michael left the sports field to take Jaymi back to the dorm for his bath, they also had a run in with the sixth form students, who also saw Michael return to the field alone.

We are not quite there yet though, David Walton is certainly looking like the who, but have you worked out the why? All the clues to that are there too, although it may have taken a little more of a leap to piece together.

The other little point to note here, although I could have mentioned it earlier, is the spelling of the choirmaster's name, Mr Sheppard. I have just Googled, and it is an occupational name of Anglo-Saxon decent with several derivatives… blah… blah… blah…

I definitely misspelled what should have been Mr Shepherd. My spelling was, and possibly still is, atrocious and I am extremely glad to be attempting my first publication during the age of autocorrect. It seems as I am drawing nearer to the end of this project, I am becoming more and more filled with self-doubt.

I mentioned several pages ago that I may reach out with a synopsis and a few chapters to a publisher, but I have yet to do so. Possibly deterred by fear of rejection but I haven't invested all this energy just to compile a private memoir, so I will have to bite the bullet at some point. I remembered I know a published author through Instagram, Clayton Littlewood, and I thought I would reach out for a little advice from him.

I became aware of Clayton through his ex-partner, Charlie Garrett, a great tattoo artist from the USA. I met him through Instagram, and we got along after sharing a few likes on each other's photos and have the occasional catchup still. I nearly met them both in London one Christmas when they were over, but work meetings got in the way.

Clayton used to live in England and his first book is a diary of tales from his shop in Soho, I recommend you check him out, and Charlie too if you are ever in Annapolis, Maryland and fancy a tattoo. I am promised one, if ever I visit, to add to the seven I already have.

Back to the advice. I sent Clayton a polite enquiry and he responded very swiftly with some good tips. The new plan is to complete this work, review again myself, ask selected friends to read and feedback thoughts or errors, revise again before seeking a professional editor/proofreader/agent that could help me get published. If all that fails, I will at least have a professionally edited book I can seek to self-publish.

So, I am single again after a reasonably long relationship with David, and feeling a bit low about the whole thing, so I do what any normal person would do and get my penis pierced. I had been thinking about it for a while and now seemed as good a time as any. Dave had been in the spare room for a couple of months while waiting for student accommodation to be allocated at Brookes, and I wasn't yet in the mood for seeing anyone else so being out of action for a while was not going to be a problem.

Turns out, due to the sterile nature of urine when it exits the body, a Prince Albert piercing is one of the fastest to heal and remarkably pain free, with the exception of the stomach-churning moment the piercer sticks a needle through your bell-end. There is also some discomfort as you stretch up through the ring gauges to your desired size but it's not too bad, I highly recommend it.

I think as a late comer to the gay scene I deliberately set out to absorb all the experiences I felt I had missed out on. I did have one tattoo while I was 'straight', but I now have seven, and I had seven piercings at one stage too, now down to just three, a nipple, the Prince Albert and my guiche.

The other thing I liked to do as often as possible was go out to the gay bars and clubs and it was on one of these weekends, sometime after the PA was healed, that I met Scott.

I had ventured out with a few friends including a couple, Dan & Mark, who had been fairly close with me and Dave. They had also arranged to meet up with some other friends, one of whom was Scott. We all met up in The Brewery Gate, the predominantly lesbian bar of the Oxford gay scene at the time. Of the three on offer it was the only one with a pool table so that probably explains it. Oh, keep your hair on, I am only joking.

We had a good night, ending up in The Plush Lounge, and rolled back home from Oxford on the night bus around 3am. I went home alone and there had been no obvious sign of any alternate offer from Scott, but he did pop up on my Grindr. I had succumbed to downloading it, just to make some new friends you understand.

We repeated the night out the following weekend, again going home alone, but on the Sunday morning Scott messaged me asking if I wanted to fuck. I wanted to, and we did. Who said romance was dead?

Scott was in his twenties, sixteen years younger than me, and a very handsome young man. I had no real expectation this was going to be a relationship but there was no reason not to just enjoy what was currently on offer. I had no idea if we would even hook up again, but I hadn't had a Sunday like that for a long time. Any day of the week for that matter.

I remember calling Dan to tell him what had happened. You'll never guess who's been around to mine, I proudly asked him. What? Why would he come around to yours? Dan clearly thought I was punching above my weight. It also turned out there was some history between them and, sadly, I think that was the start of the end of our friendship.

There were other factors too. Dan and my ex, Dave, slipping off to the rocks in Mykonos for some holiday fun with strangers one evening when I had gone back to my room early. Dave had let that slip after we split up, he had forgotten I didn't know and seemed rather embarrassed when I picked him up on it, but it was water under the bridge by then.

Dan and Dave had also been very good friends, and Scott was a completely different character who had no intention of replacing Dave in the routines and customs we had got used to, so things changed there too. However, before the event that was the final straw of that friendship, we would all go away on holiday together. A long weekend in Barcelona and then a week on the beach down the coast in Sitges.

Despite my low expectations, it turned out that Scott and I were getting on really well and seeing each other regularly, so I had made the offer of a free holiday to him, which he gladly accepted. This was the holiday Dave did not want to come on and there was only a small fee to change the name on the ticket. There were seven of us due to go so I let them know I was going to be bringing someone after all. Coincidentally, all these years later, three of the guys from that holiday are coming up to visit this weekend.

It was a great holiday both in Barcelona and Sitges. We started with the weekend in Barcelona and by pure chance it happened to be Pride weekend, so we partied. One of our group had a camera stolen and another their wallet, although in defence of the infamous Barcelona pickpockets, the wallet could easily have just slipped out on a dark room floor. Dom, you know it's true.

The Sitges week was more chilled, plenty of drinking of an evening, with more relaxing days on the beach. I had holidayed with this group before when with Dave and it was always very enjoyable, but Scott wasn't Dave, and despite his younger years, he was more confident and less compliant than I would have usually been. After a couple of nights of trying to agree where to eat as a group, or which bar to go into, usually as a result of Dan's fussiness, Scott spoke up.

Not recalling the exact words, the message was along the lines of 'You do what you want to do, we'll do what we want to do, and we will see you later'. Another black mark in Dan's book against Scott's name, though I know at least a couple of the others in the group appreciated Scott's interjection.

It didn't spoil the holiday, not for us at least, and I enjoyed my fortieth birthday on the gay beach in Sitges drinking champagne and eating cream cakes with a great bunch of guys. I had a hot boyfriend, and he was showing me a different approach to gay life which I was enjoying very much. Unfortunately, not everything Scott opened my eyes to was positive and we were heading for a couple of stumbles.

About a year after Sitges, we were due to go on holiday again to Cyprus with a couple of Scott's friends, when I discovered he had been seeing someone else. Not only seeing but had actually secured this person a job so they now worked together. It wasn't the first time, but it was more serious now as we were living together. We had taken it slow and not moved in together quickly, but now that we had, I assumed we were monogamous, although our relationship was still barely a year old.

For those in the dark, I think it is fairly common for gay couples to have open relationships. Nothing wrong with this but we hadn't discussed it, I was pretty sure I didn't want an open relationship, and I was certain I didn't want a half-open one. I confided in Dan and Mark who were outraged on my behalf, however, I decided it wasn't over and we may as well still go on the holiday.

The holiday was okay, a little tense, but we made it through. The friendship with Dan and Mark died there though. They were incensed I had cried on their shoulders but had not taken their advice. To this day I am not sure what I personally did wrong. Years later I met Dan for a conciliatory coffee, but we could only agree to disagree. I do miss their friendship, or at least how it was when I was with Dave. I don't think it would ever have been the same with Scott, regardless of his infidelities.

The next three years were full of fun and adventure and, although they would end with more medical drama and heartache, they started well. On our return from Cyprus, we picked up our new puppy, Mason, son of Macy, the dog belonging to Scott's Mum. Mason, who will be ten this September, is currently at my feet as I type these words, alas little Macy had to be put to sleep only last week due to failing health.

We took in a lodger at one point too, Matt, a gay guy we knew following a fun and somewhat naughty night away in Cheltenham. He lived with us for around three months, so he could take a job in Oxford, before getting his own place. Good times!

Maria and Frank, Scott's mother and stepfather lived in Burford where Scott had grown up and we used to spend a good amount of time there ourselves. Following yet another taxi ride back home one evening, the idea was floated about buying a house there. We moved into our cottage almost seven months later after an unnecessarily painful purchase process, at one point looking like we may lose the property, but it all came right in the end.

Life was good. The house needed a reasonable amount of work inside and out and we busied ourselves with DIY and gardening. There were also some major jobs required on the bathroom and windows, but everything moved along at pace, and we were soon enjoying our new home and a very social life in Burford. I remember recording a video of myself walking home from our local, The Cotswold Arms, and the length of the video from door-to-door was two minutes fifty-nine seconds. Impressive in itself but there are actually seven other bars closer to our cottage than this one.

Our other great love was travelling, and we were fortunate to be able to take a couple of overseas holidays each year, possibly the odd weekend away too. Mykonos was our absolute favourite, returned to several times, but we liked to see other places too. I have also been fortunate to travel with work and one of these trips was to a conference in New York. I did not expect to be a fan but absolutely loved the trip so shortly afterwards, for Scott's birthday, I booked us a Christmas shopping weekend for early December.

We stayed in a lovely boutique hotel just off Times Square and it was another great trip. We visited all the tourist attractions you would expect, and also hooked up for lunch with my nephew and his wife who were living there at the time. We visited a great bar in the Meat Packing District on their recommendation, Flaming Saddles, which is basically the gay version of the bar from the film *Coyote Ugly*, where the barmen dance on the bar top every ten minutes or so. However, the best event of our long weekend was still to come.

The tourist trail took us to the Empire State Building, no surprise there, but when we were at the very top viewing platform, with snow blowing around us, Scott proposed to me. It was a total surprise but very welcome and very romantic. Later that day he also took me to Tiffany's, 5th Avenue and purchased matching engagement rings. Of course, for the superstitious amongst us, when everything is going this well, in the yin-yang of life it is only a matter of time before another challenge crops up.

While out one day in New York I was talking to Scott and my vision went blurry, just for a second, and I could tell something strange had happened by the look on Scott's face. He described to me that my right eye had moved completely to the right of the socket before moving back to the centre. This happened again a couple of times while we were away, only becoming worse on our return, so I decided to go to the optician in the first instance to see what was going on.

The optician had immediate concerns and advised it was beyond his expertise and suggested I go to my GP with some urgency. The GP had similar concerns and I was referred to the eye hospital which luckily, I was able to do privately through my work medical insurance. It took almost three months from first incident to diagnosis, with very worrying periods of waiting for brain tumour scan results and the like. The condition worsened and began to impact both eyes but luckily it was not a brain tumour, and my final diagnosis was Ocular Myasthenia Gravis (OMG!).

OMG is an autoimmune disease affecting the muscles that control movement of the eyes. The wider condition can affect muscles elsewhere in the body and become very debilitating but for me the impact was limited to the ocular variant. Once diagnosed treatment began with a course of steroids which builds gradually to a large dose until the condition is under control, before then reducing the dose again to a low level over another very long period of time, ensuring the condition does not return at any point. It has been seven years and I am still on a very low dose of steroids, though luckily, I have never experienced a relapse.

This whole period was very stressful, firstly due to the uncertainty of the condition and then because of the time taken to get the condition under control. I had to wear a patch and driving was difficult with only vision from one eye. There is always humour of course, either eye would work fine alone but they were not aligned to work together. The advice was to wear a patch but swap it from eye to eye every couple of hours. I am sure work colleagues were puzzled when I told them I had a bad eye but the next time they walked by my desk the patch had swapped sides.

Alongside this medical stress there were also changes afoot at the company I was working for, Mothercare, and the future there did not look overly secure and was causing further anxiety. Worse still, almost a year to the day from our lovely New York engagement, Scott and I would split up.

We had an almighty row on the day I was leaving for a work trip to Hong Kong and India, punctuated by me leaving my engagement ring on the side as I walked out the door. By the time I returned the situation had become critical.

In the months prior, Scott had been spending time with friends outside of our joint circle and while I was away one of these friendships crossed the line. However, I need to put my hands up at this point and say I almost certainly drove him to it. I will try to explain.

We moved house, we were holidaying, we were socialising, we had an engagement party on our return from New York and all was well on the surface but behind closed doors our relationship remained under stress. I was definitely the cause of this stress, and I can say that quite confidently with the benefit of hindsight and offer a little advice to anyone who goes through something similar. If you decide to get back together with someone who has cheated on you, then you need to be able to let it go.

I did not let it go. I would find myself throwing the pre-Cyprus incident in Scott's face every time we had the slightest disagreement, even three years after it had occurred in the very early stages of our relationship. I can't really explain other than to say it had been a very hurtful event, but now it was me perpetuating the misery. We had agreed we wanted to be together, but I was no longer making that possible. I wasn't a very nice person for a while there, I am not even sure why Scott wanted to propose to me, maybe he thought the gesture would stop me being so obsessively jealous.

Love and heartache are very complicated, and it was going to get a little more complicated yet. We didn't split up straight away, we even hosted a family Christmas that year, 2014, and despite Scott now seeing another guy we also agreed to go out together with a mutual girlfriend over the holiday period. That was a mistake.

I am not going to go in to all the details, but the end result of the evening was a fight between myself and Scott which, quite frustratingly, resulted in our friend calling the police and us both being arrested and spending a night in the cells. After sobering up and cooling down, we were both released at the same time and Scott called Frank and he came and picked us both up and took us home.

It was a strange period. We never quite recovered the relationship with the friend who had called the police that night although, in a further bizarre twist, she is now living with Michael, the best man from my wedding to Jill. They were due to get married this year, but I am not sure if COVID intervened. Contact between myself and Michael is fairly limited these days, but I will see him again, I'm sure.

I think the shock of the police involvement calmed us both, but it wasn't enough to reverse the course of events. The day came for Scott to move out and there were tears from both of us. It was heartbreakingly sad, and I was single again.

CHAPTER 15

Coles and Bradey walked slowly into the room, stopping a few feet from the window when David threatened to jump.

'Come back inside,' Bradey said softly. 'It won't help anyone if you jump.'

'I won't go to prison,' David justified.

'McWinney was a bad piece of work, they'll understand that.'

'What about Jaymi though? I killed him as well you know.'

'Why did you do it?' Coles asked.

'My brother used to go to this school a long time ago. He died of an overdose because of someone like McWinney. When I found out he was a dealer I followed him until I got some pictures of him dealing. I confronted him up here, but I didn't mean to kill him. I thought I could threaten him into stopping, but when I got here, he was so smug. It was like looking at my brother's killer. I couldn't stop myself.'

'Stuart Walton? Was he your brother?' Bradey asked, remembering the printout on the previous drug problems at the school. The one Coles had told him to 'file'.

David nodded before continuing his confession.

'I was emptying the mail when Jaymi came up to me and gave me a letter to post. I opened it and read that he had seen me upstairs. I was scarred so I killed him to cover my tracks. I deserve this,' David said as he edged forward on to the ledge.

'The boy who wrote the letter,' Bradey said. 'He hadn't seen you upstairs, he had seen Mr Price.'

'So, I killed him for nothing?'

'Worse than that I'm afraid, Jaymi didn't even write the letter. He was just posting it for a friend.'

David could not believe what he was hearing. He had started to cry and bowed his head into his hands. Bradey rushed forward when David's eyes were covered and grabbed him back inside the room.

David's tears ran faster, and he turned to Bradey for help. Bradey comforted him as they left the room and walked down the stairs to the car.

They drove back to the station in silence and spent the rest of the day doing the necessary paperwork.

'You did well to pull him back in from the edge,' Coles complimented when he and Bradey were alone.

'Thank you,' Bradey replied. 'I really felt sorry for him. Do you think they'll be lenient?'

'I don't think so, maybe for McWinney but for Jaymi, not a chance.'

The two of them walked to their cars together, exchanged farewells, and then headed for home.

Coles put his car in the garage then went inside. Martin had fallen asleep on the settee waiting for his father to come home. Coles switched off the television and carried his son upstairs. Martin barely stirred as Coles undressed him and put him to bed. Coles had a quick shower before going back downstairs to get himself a sandwich and a cold beer.

As he sat at the kitchen table, he noticed the tickets to the Christmas concert. Each was headed with the school's coat of arms and Coles read aloud the motto that scrolled across the base of the shield 'Domus Innocentiae'. He smiled at the irony and vowed that the concert would be his last visit to the school.

Coles and his son were seated near the front of the church. Neither had ever been a great lover of choir music but both were enjoying themselves.

The concert was nearing the interval and Coles suggested they go and have a drink. As the last song finished, they made their way to the back room where refreshments were being served. Coles purchased two teas with accompanying biscuits and sat with his son in a corner of the room. After a short time, they courteously gave up their seats to an elderly couple and were left standing for the remainder of the interval. For the first time, for as long as Coles could remember, Martin asked him how work was.

After the initial shock of the question Coles decided to give a brief answer and avoid dwelling on the subject that had caused so much pain in their relationship.

'Oh! Just finishing up the paperwork.'

Instead of changing the subject Martin continued with obvious interest.

'What happened then? Who did it?'

'Well, one boy killed a man because he was selling drugs. The boy's brother died of an overdose, and I suppose he didn't want the same thing to happen to anyone else.'

'Didn't two people get killed?' Martin probed.

'Yes, a young lad was killed because the murderer thought he was a witness.'

'Well, you caught the killer, and the drug dealer is dead, so it wasn't all bad. Everyone else will be safer.'

'That's my job,' Coles smiled at his son's innocence. 'Anyway, have you thought any more about boarding school?'

'Yes,' Martin replied. 'I don't want to go.'

Coles smiled again.

The second section of the concert began with the choir master, Mr Sheppard, introducing Michael to the stage. He informed the audience that he was not usually a member of the choir but was best friends with Jaymi, the student tragically taken from them all, and had asked if he could sing a small part in memory of his friend.

The music started and Michael, assisted by one of the other boys, sang the opening bars from a piece called *Sing Forever*.

'I will sing for you at the start of each day, I'll sing forever, sing for you'.

The sombre audience listened intently. It wouldn't have mattered how Michael had sounded but it was actually beautiful, he had practiced his opening line as he wanted to do his best for

Jaymi. The rest of the choir accompanied the remainder of the song and there was not a dry eye in the house. Coles held Martin's hand tightly for the length of the performance, only releasing it at the end to wipe a tear from his own cheek.

On the far side of the school the sound of the choir could be heard softly filling the corridors. It was the same angelic sound that Price had heard on the morning of McWinney's death that he heard again now, for the last time, as he kicked away the chair from beneath his feet.

For a moment, the sound of the choir was drowned out by the clattering of the chair as it fell to the ground, but when the chair settled the echoes of a boy could be heard, once more accompanied by the creaking of the noose.

On the table to the side of where Price's lifeless body hung was a note waiting to be found. It read:

> My career and my marriage are over,
> my life may as well be.
> Sorry.

ANALYSIS 15

So here we are, you've made it to the end of my Murder at St Philip's story, originally written in 1987 when I was a seventeen-year-old boy but only now, thirty-four years later, being shared with the world. How was it for you? Actually, don't tell me, I don't think I can take the rejection.

For me it all seemed to get tied up very quickly over the last two chapters, almost an anti-climax after all the posturing, but the Walton link was there to be found starting all the way back in the pivotal broken tape-recorder chapter. Admittedly you'd have had to guess they were brothers when the second Walton reference came along but the nature of their relationship wasn't critical, just that they were related.

I also recall that when David Walton took the letter from Jaymi, Mr Price was also present so that could also have explained why he might have had it in his possession and burned it in his office fireplace. When most of the clues were dropped there was also a decoy element. I think it worked. I could be wrong.

The concert section with Michael singing for his dead friend is for me another scene I can visualise in great detail playing out on screen. I would want it to be heart-breaking and I would have panned the cameras out of the church, across the whole school as the music was playing, and back through the window to Price's office. The choir would still be singing when Price kicked away the chair with the cameras final focus falling on the suicide note as the credits began to roll.

I really like the ending with Price committing suicide. I am not a great lover of happy endings, so this works for me, the crime is solved but there are no real winners. It crossed my mind when I re-read this finale if the suicide of the 'outed' gay man was any kind of reflection on how I may have been feeling about my own sexuality, an explanation for the subsequent years of suppression. I wrote this story around the same time my friend Ian rejected the advances of my love letter, scratching me from his life. I'm no psychologist but there could be a link.

With regard to closing everything off neatly, I am not interested in the consequences of the suicide, or even the outcome of any prosecution of David Walton, the story was intended to be a snapshot of a crime. It isn't even about a genius Morse-like detective solving a great mystery, just a simple journey through the events until we arrive at the truth of the matter. Sometimes life is just shit.

Life isn't always shit though. I have another confession to make, I lied at the end of the last part of my biography, I never split up with Scott and our story does have a happy ending. Don't get me wrong, he did move out and we were apart for around four months but looking back on that time now, we were always together. This is going to take a little explaining.

Scott moved out some time in the new year of 2015 and was now seeing another guy. I had no real concern that this new relationship would be anything long term, but it was upsetting to think he had moved on so quickly. In response I took to the dreaded Grindr and, I am neither proud nor ashamed to say, I slept around. This was very out of character for me and in this four-month period I slept with more people than the entire rest of my life. I enjoyed it too, not all of them, but most.

If there is a positive to be taken from the whole experience, for the first time in my life I realised there is a difference between love and sex. I know that sounds naive, especially for the forty-four-year-old man I was at the time, but I had never previously separated the two. Don't get me wrong, I am not trying to justify misbehaviour, explain away open relationships, or excuse any adulterers but it did help me come to understand how these things can be overcome and how you can reconcile a relationship without being bitter and vindictive, as I fear I had been too many occasions previously.

When I had been with Jill, and Sian before that, in my previous life, there had never been any question of staying together once the unfaithfulness had occurred. But I had already overcome this once with Scott and even now, all I really wanted was for him to come back home. Scott was special for sure and at risk of sounding crass, not for the first time, the four months apart opened my eyes as much as my thighs!

Scott stopped seeing his new fella for various reasons, which remain his business, and he came around for a drink one evening to tell me about it and I genuinely thought he was going to ask me to get back with him. Instead, he explained how an old friend had got back in touch, and they had hit it off and were seeing each other a bit. Gutted!

While I just knew the previous guy was a non-starter, this seemed like a much bigger threat to any recovery of our own relationship, but we were getting along better now, and I told Scott I was happy for him. I started to socialise a bit more myself too, a combination of crying on my friend Lynn's shoulder and going out swimming, or to the sauna or cinema with Gareth, a friend I had reconnected with.

For the record, Gareth was not one of the guys I slept with. I didn't really know him overly well, he was more a friend of a friend, but he was also going through a relationship breakup, and we had started talking and I think we just liked each other and enjoyed the company.

I haven't spoken to Gareth as much since he reconciled with his partner, but I was aware they had separated again. I know he also lost his father, to whom he was very close, and I did message my condolences at the time. After reaching out again recently, prompted by all this reminiscing, he sent me a picture of the cutest little lad he is now fostering. Gareth is just the loveliest man, but I'll stop now, spare any more of his blushes.

I am guessing this all sounds very terminal with regard to my relationship with Scott, but again I have been a little light with the truth of that whole four-month period. At no point did we stop talking to each other, at no point did we stop seeing each other, and at no point did we stop sleeping together.

Early on there was still some tension but even then, we might be together once, twice, even three times a week. We started to get along better again, and I bought him a little something for his birthday that March. Then one day, towards the end of April, Scott came over to tell me he had separated with the old friend he had started to see. He wasn't enjoying himself. He was doing a lot of running around and doing things he didn't really like. I would love to tell you he had an epiphany and begged me to take him back, but it wasn't quite like that.

We seemed to be spending every evening together now and this quickly developed into staying the night, every night. One morning I just asked him outright, 'Are we back together now?'. It seemed we were, so we bit the bullet, he moved his stuff back in, and we went public on our reconciliation. I was really touched by our friend's reaction to us getting back together, it seemed everyone liked us as a couple.

Early in the May we booked a weekend away to Torremolinos for a little rest and relaxation. We had a really nice break and I have just had a few photos pop up on my social media memories as it is now the sixth anniversary of that trip. Later that year we also took another little trip to London for a works Christmas party. We were staying the night in a hotel, and I had snuck along our engagement rings in my luggage. I re-presented them to Scott after a couple of afternoon drinks and we wore them out for the meal that evening. All was good in the world again.

The next four years were packed full of all sorts of experiences, more holidays, parties, threesomes, poppers, Pride concerts fuelled sometimes by a little more than alcohol. It was Britney, bitch! You needed to be high.

But now, staying firmly on the right side of the law, let me pick out a few of the highlights and lowlights before we arrive at 19th September 2019, by far the greatest day of my life.

One of the first things that happened after we got back together had the potential to be quite worrying but, in the end, worked out very well for me. Mothercare, my employer at the time, decided to restructure and my position no longer existed. I was offered an alternate role, but it would have been a downwards step which did not interest me at all. Luckily, there was an offer of an enhanced redundancy package, which I cannot discuss as it was signed under NDA through my solicitor, but through a combination of length of service and the enhanced elements it was extremely attractive. I also managed to walk straight into another job, so it was all a bit of a bonus really. I did some sensible things with the money, and I bought a sports car and a Jacuzzi too. You have to live a little.

We continued with our love of holidaying and visited all sorts of places. Ibiza, Hong Kong, Berlin, Gran Canaria, Mykonos, Santorini, Vienna, Paris, Barcelona, Sardinia, as well as a few UK weekends away too. We even did a first and holidayed separately, something I couldn't imagine the old me being comfortable with at all.

Scott went on a trip with a girl friend to The Dominican Republic, taking the place of her ex-boyfriend, while I hopped on a jump-seat to Cairo with a great friend, Geraint, who was rather handily a British Airways cabin manager. I say jump-seat, he bumped me to Business Class on the way out and on the way back I experienced life as a 1A First Class bitch. Love you Daddy G.

We faced some tough times too, by far the worst of which was the loss of Scott's grandfather, shortly after his grandmother was taken in to care due to her deteriorating health. Scott surprised me with how strong he was throughout, he should be very proud of how he handled himself and I know his grandfather would have been proud of him too, to know he carried him to his final resting place.

As you become older, events such as funerals start you questioning your own mortality and reminiscing about the things you have done, or equally haven't done, and questioning if you should do something about it before it is too late. While writing these pages I have reached out to several of the old friends I talk about, mostly just a brief 'hello', but it would be good to reconnect some of these friendships more permanently.

One of the friendships I did manage to reach out and reconnect, almost three years ago now, was with Darren Hall, my first ever teenage crush. It is a bittersweet tale I will tell you now.

I had tried to find Darren online a few times over the years with no success. Firstly, back in the Friends Reunited days and then at intervals on various social sites but always to no avail. Then one day, while trying again, a new face seemed to pop up on the list of Darren Halls Facebook had to offer. It wasn't instant recognition but there was a hint of familiarity, so I stalked a bit further. I scrolled back through the profile pictures and suddenly there was the face I remembered. He had uploaded a picture of himself as a teenager.

I messaged Darren on 5th June 2018 via Facebook messenger. I have just read back the message and it was amazingly honest, considering our time together had been brief, not to mention thirty-two years previous. I gave him a very quick recap on our time together and a few of my life highlights since. I told him how profound meeting him had been for me and how he had never been forgotten, even confessing he had been my first crush. I sent him a picture of myself back then as an aide memoire, but I had opened my message, '…you probably don't remember…' so he had an easy get out to close down this conversation. Assuming he would reply at all.

He replied and it was just lovely. Darren was not at all offended to have been my crush, flattered in fact he said, but tragically he did not remember me. He went on to explain his life had been a rollercoaster, to say the least, and he was dealing with a lot of physical and psychological issues that had all but destroyed his memory.

In 2012 Darren was hit by a car while living in Germany and was left severely disabled after undergoing years of surgery. This came on top of a spina bifida diagnosis in his late teens which ended his professional football career at Swindon Town. The trauma also caused severe memory loss as well as early-onset dementia.

I am not speaking out of turn here as Darren has recently disclosed this information in a local newspaper article about his artwork. He has always loved art from a young age and now he works on this full time and finds it an essential therapeutic distraction from the issues he has to deal with. I will keep to the publicly disclosed information but through the course of redeveloping our friendship Darren has shared other details, from earlier in his life, and I know he has had several other demons to deal with over the years too.

One day I found myself talking to another friend about how I had finally managed to reconnect with Darren. While explaining the original relationship, the impact it had on me, and some of the events that have occurred since, I broke down in tears. I had a terrible, irrational, feeling of guilt. What if I hadn't moved away? What if we had kept in touch? Maybe some of these awful things may not have happened.

I knew, even as a fifteen-year-old boy, Darren was having an impact on my every thought and feeling about myself and my sexuality. I also knew the move away from Abingdon was the most traumatic of my childhood as an air force nomad. What I didn't realise, until we reconnected, is I had been carrying this loss with me for years and I needed to cry it out.

I am pleased to say we are keeping in touch and although when we reconnected, Darren was living in Scotland, coincidentally he has recently moved to Oxfordshire and now lives about four miles away from me. We haven't met up yet, Darren needs to be comfortable in his own body and mind before we get there, but when it happens it will be great to have a coffee with him and just chat.

I am also the proud owner of a piece of Darren's original art, a large heart in predominantly pink. The canvas must be almost a metre square, either oil or acrylic applied with a pallet knife from my limited knowledge. It is a beautiful piece Darren gifted to Scott and me for our wedding, which brings me nicely back to 19th September 2019, the happiest day of my life.

As someone who has witnessed the birth of their child, I don't say this lightly. Of course, Aaron's birth was just amazing and clearly also one of the best days of my life but the wedding to Scott symbolised such a transition from my previous life, as well as the strength of our relationship after some difficult times.

We booked the wedding after being back together for around three years, and with around eighteen months' notice so we could secure our chosen venue. For anyone planning the same, the eighteen months flew past and there was a lot to get organised. The date was chosen accidentally, we wanted September, we wanted a Thursday, only afterwards did we realise 19/09/19 looked very good on the invitations, not to mention being easy to remember for future anniversaries!

The planning of the whole day was actually pretty exciting and not something I had ever done before as my first wedding to Jill was a very low budget registry office affair. Don't get me wrong, it was a great day spent celebrating with friends but nothing on this scale. Luckily, finances have improved since the early nineties as Scott isn't really a low budget kind of guy.

From the 'Save the Date' pre-invitations, through to the final suit fitting, we planned and agreed on all the little details of the day. There were a few challenges with the seating plan as we had to accommodate all the latest developments in the soap opera that is Burford life. Mine and Scott's relationship may have been going from strength to strength but the same was not true for some other members of our friends and family group.

Muffin couldn't sit near Alice as they used to go out. Lynn couldn't sit near Billy as they used to go out. Lynn also couldn't sit near Charlotte as she was now seeing Billy. Luckily, Rhys, as best man, was safely tucked away sitting next to his brother, as he had previously been in a long-term relationship with Charlotte. Rhys and Lynn also had some kind of rebound history as a result of the Billy and Charlotte thing. Wisely, Rhys chose not to bring his new romance

Polly as his plus one, that would have opened a whole other can of worms.

Without going in to all the details I think the easiest way to describe the day is as a wholly classic wedding. We stayed apart the night before and arrived separately in ribboned cars. I had Aaron with me as my best man and Scott had his brother Rhys. Little Ronni, my granddaughter, was our flower girl and we had a short but classic service. Champagne and canapés followed, before the wedding breakfast, speeches, and an evening of dancing to a live band, all kicked off by our first dance to a remix of Kylie Minogue's, *All the Lovers*. This had been our holiday song from our first ever holiday to Sitges, nine years previously when I had changed the name on Dave's ticket and took Scott instead. It was always our destiny.

I cannot put into words how special the whole day was. The weather was fantastic, we have such beautiful photos to go with the memories, and our friends have told us how much they all enjoyed the day. I can't really think of anything I would have done differently, and I know Scott feels the same. Relationships are not always easy and ours is no different to any other, gay, or straight. They come with challenges to be worked through together. We have had ours in the past and I am sure we will have some more in the future but that day, 19th September 2019, was a day full of pure love for each other. On lord, pass me a tissue!

The wedding almost brings us back full circle to where this project started. A week after the wedding, when I returned to work after a short break to Sitges as a little mini-moon, I was introduced to the new CTO. There began the worst six months of my working career, and a chain of events started which would lead to me revisiting my writing and working on this whole project as some feeble means of escape.

Ironically, a combination of the COVID pandemic and CTO maternity leave came as some form of reprieve for me personally, and I do not make light at all of the pandemic and the huge impact and loss this has brought for many. But for me it has been an enjoyable experience, continuing to work and therefore get paid.

I have spent a lot more quality time with my husband, Scott, who has been furloughed for the majority of the last year. His brother, Rhys, who has been living with us throughout the various lockdown periods was also furloughed, however, his skills as a chef have been put to great use and my waistline is testament to that.

Rhys has also been good company as a drinking buddy and I've got to know him a lot more, although he wisely didn't attend my lockdown fiftieth, at which I was treated to a stripper the girls had organised for me. It was a sunny Sunday afternoon in a Burford beer garden, but to my surprise he didn't let that stop him going all the way. He had clearly pre-fluffed and tied himself off a bit too tight. It may have been big, but it did not look healthy at all. I see now why they use the aubergine emoji as a representation.

Workwise, the subsequent news of the CTO not returning to the company has somewhat reignited my work flame, however, as lockdown restrictions come to an end, our company strategy seems to be to get everyone back to the office. With only a token home working policy introduced so far, my flame is at risk of being dampened a little once more, but it is a step forward and I am optimistic more positive change will come.

And there you have it. I will now re-read and re-edit these pages with a view to sharing with some trusted friends for their feedback. I will then, if not mortally deflated, seek professional assistance to try and get this project published and in front of your eyes. If I fail you will never know, and if I have succeeded, I hope you have enjoyed this little insight into my adult life as well as the teenage fiction from the echoes of a boy.

AFTERWORD

I thought I should take a little bit of time to review my own work and see if I have managed to achieve my objective when I started this project. It is currently early June 2021, so I have taken just over five months to complete my venture, although as yet nobody else has read any of these pages. I may add a little section to the end of the afterword with some feedback from the first person I allow to review it. I can't even decide who that should be at the moment. My husband seems an obvious choice, however, I am inclined to ask someone more independent in the first instance.

As a reminder of the original concept, basically I was unhappy in my job and had decided to revisit an old ambition I held to be a writer. While considering ideas for potential story lines, I had this crazy idea to take the original manuscript of an unpublished novella I had written as a teenager, and around it I would weave the story of my life. Along the way I would explain how my early life experiences had influenced the story telling, but as three-fifths of my life have occurred after the story was completed, it would also be an interesting exercise in how my boyhood and adolescent experiences have gone on to shape and influence the man I am today.

I quipped at the idea in the preface, and have hinted throughout, I have no idea if this concept is going to be of any interest to anyone other than myself. It is usual that you earn the right to publish a biography of your life through achievements in one field or another, usually in the public eye. I have had a successful career, but it is very much a mundane one, out of the public eye. No movie star, no pop star, no politician, not even an author, just an anonymous IT manager.

In terms of how I have delivered on my task, the original manuscript is all there in full, giving some insight into my ability at the time. I like some of it, I am embarrassed by some of it, but it is what it is. I would still love to see it on the screen, I had such a vision in my head at the time.

I have also explained the background of some of the characters and some of my early experiences which clearly shaped some of the scenes of the story, so I think I have ticked that box too.

The third thread was the onward biography of my later years, after the St Philip's story was complete. On reflection this isn't really a biography of my life, I have skipped over so many things, instead it is very much a focused biography on my relationships and ultimately my coming out as a gay man. I am happy enough with this though, maybe I will get another chance to talk about the wider aspects of my life another time.

I am conscious there is a strong theme of sexual awaking throughout the fictional and biographical elements, but I think this is merely a reflection of my life. I began writing this story as pubescent boy exploring his sexuality, which remained unresolved for another seventeen years.

I mentioned I like to post underwear pictures on my Instagram account, amongst other more mainstream insights into my life, but this is not really a new interest for me. I received a camera for my eighteenth birthday and have always liked to take nude photographs of myself, even back in the days when you had to have your films developed at Boots, or by post with TruPrint or the like.

I still have a small collection of photos from that time and if this book ever makes it to print, I have already created a cover which includes a naked picture of myself, artistically filtered for modesty, taken some time between the ages of eighteen and twenty I would guess. Another echo from the past, more echoes of a boy, of me as a boy. I toyed with several titles, but Echoes of a Boy works well for me.

I am also conscious that I have mentioned several people from my life, and none have been consulted. I hope none will be offended, even the work-related comments are not intended to offend, only to explain my state of mind at the time this project was conceived.

Ironically, my work life has improved considerably through the course of these writings, and I am reinvigorated and enjoying work again. And of course, this is by nature a one-sided account of events, my own memories, my own interpretation, my own assumptions. It doesn't mean I am right.

Risks of libel aside, I remain optimistically eager to publish, and my thoughts are already turning to ideas for my next venture. I have another story I started just a little later than the St Philip's one, nowhere near as complete but there is an opening chapter and an outline for the plot. It is a horror of sorts, set in and around the area I was living at the time, so I may well revisit this and see if I can make something of it.

But for now, I am pleased to have come to the end of this first project, thirty-four years in the making. I have stretched out this draft manuscript to around seventy thousand words over almost three hundred pages and I am happy with the result. I now look forward to sharing it and taking some professional advice. Of course, if you are reading this I will have already done so, and you will have just finished reading the polished version. If you have made it this far, thank you so much, I hope you have enjoyed my ramblings.

ACKNOWLEDGEMENTS

Jason Curtis, my chosen first victim to read this book. This was not a random choice, I did it with the best intentions, I hope it helped.

Kirsten Curry, a fellow KDP published author *(The Kiki Leeton Mysteries)*. Thank you so much for your advice and your red pen skills, which were much needed!

Scott Godfray-Hoare, I should have let you read it before I published the first edition, but I was too impatient. Lesson learnt, corrections made, and now you have also made it into the acknowledgements! xXx

Printed in Great Britain
by Amazon